The Merry Muses of

Robert Burns

THE MERRY MUSES

OF

CALEDONIA;

(ORIGINAL EDITION)

A COLLECTION OF
FAVOURITE SCOTS SONGS
ANCIENT AND MODERN;
SELECTED FOR USE OF THE

CROCHALLAN FENCIBLES.

> Say, Puritan, can it be wrong,
> To dress plain truth in witty song?
> What honest Nature says, we should do;
> What every lady does... or would do.

A VINDICATION
OF ROBERT BURNS
IN CONNECTION WITH THE ABOVE PUBLICATION
AND
THE SPURIOUS EDITIONS WHICH SUCCEEDED IT.

CONTENTS.

(AS IN THE ORIGINAL.)

———

INTRODUCTORY AND CORRECTIVE

APART from his genius, Robert Burns is the most prominent figure of his time in the history of the ballad and song literature of Scotland. The extent, variety, and accuracy of his knowledge in this particular walk is the more remarkable when it is considered that few facilities existed in his day for the study of the subject; and these were, moreover, so fragmentary and loosely connected as to be almost valueless. In fact, the literature of Scottish song can scarcely be said to have made a beginning till after the second decade of the eighteenth century, when Allan Ramsay gave an impetus to the native lyric, which, continued through the Jacobite period, reached its culmination in the era of Burns, and can scarcely be said to have yet expended itself. The ancient Scots "Makaris" eschewed the lyric as unworthy of their muse; and at a later period the clergy set their faces steadfastly to destroy the indigenous growth of song by the substitution of "gude and godlie ballates," which, whatever may be thought of them otherwise, served the good end of preserving the old titles and measures. Cropped at the surface, the national poesy struck its roots into the subsoil and became a wilding of bye-paths and shady places, of vigorous growth, rank, and luxuriant. There Burns found it; tended, pruned, engrafted, and transplanted it; till, from the corrupting stock of ribaldry, obscenity, and licentiousness, he feasted the world with the fruits of Hesperides. He employed no labourer; he did the navvy work himself. Small wonder is it, then, that the skirts of his mantle shew some traces of the scavenger work which was the self-imposed task of his life. On this point, Robert Chambers, in his *Life and Works* of the Poet, out of the fulness and ripeness of his knowledge, writes:—

"With a strange contradiction to the grave and religious character of the Scottish people, they possessed a wonderful quantity of indecorous traditionary verse, not of an inflammatory character, but simply expressive of a profound sense of the ludicrous in connection with the sexual affections. Such things, usually kept from public view, oozed out in merry companies such as Burns loved to frequent. Men laughed at them for the moment, and in the sober daylight of next morning had forgotten them. When our poet was particularly struck by any free-spoken ditty of the old school he would scribble it down and transfer it to a commonplace book. In time, what he thus collected he was led to imitate, apparently for no other object than that of amusing his merry companions in their moments of conviviality. … I am, nevertheless, convinced that his conduct originated mainly in nothing worse than his strong sense of the ludicrous. Of this, I venture to say, there could be no doubt entertained by the public if it were allowable to bring the proper evidence into Court. It is also to be admitted that, to heighten the effect, he was too apt to bring in a dash of levity respecting Scriptural characters and incidents—a kind of bad taste, however, for which an example was set to him in the common conversation of his countrymen; for certain it is that the piety of the old Scottish people did not exclude a very considerable share of what may be called an unconscious profanity."   In boyhood and early youth, we are told, he consumed with eager mind-hunger everything that partook of the complexion of his genius, and when the slender stores at his command were exhausted he betook himself to the volume of traditionary lore written on the memories of the men and women around him; chronicling with faithful pen all their uncouth utterances—eliminating, restoring, amending—till the crooked was made straight and the rough places plain. Every one conversant with Burns's literary methods well knows that the discovery of a ballad or song in his autograph is no conclusive proof, *per se*, that he is the author of it. He was continually noting down every echo of the elder Scottish Muse that was carried to his ear, and "high-kilted was she," indeed, if her presentment everywhere is anything like an approximate portrait. All was fish that came into the net, to be preserved as suggestions for Johnson and Thomson in the private manuscript referred to, of which more anon. Copies of the more amusing "Cloaciniads,"[1] however, were dispatched forthwith (yet not without the precaution of privacy) to the jesters of the Crochallan Club, or hastily jotted down for future reference on odd scraps of paper, as the old version of "Bonie Dundee" on the reverse of the Earl of Buchan's letter in the Poet's Monument, Edinburgh, exemplifies; and these confidences, we do not hesitate to say, in not a few instances, have been since used in a way that is as disgraceful as it is dishonourable to all concerned. Nor can the dictum of any editor, however able and erudite, be accepted as final, unless some more satisfactory evidence is produced than the assumed Burns flavour of the ballad or song itself. Yet, in face of these considerations, many pieces—and these mostly of the objectionable sort—have passed into currency as compositions of Burns, whose claims to that distinction rest solely on evidence of the flimsy character indicated. Even such a strong presumption of authenticity as unchallenged publication during the Poet's lifetime is open to grave suspicion, seeing that he himself thus writes to Thomson in November, 1794:—

"I myself have lately seen a couple of ballads sung through the streets of Dumfries with my name at the head of them as the author though it was the first time I had ever seen them."

Thomson himself (Sept., 1793,) falls into the error of supposing that the free-spoken ditty, "The other night with all her charms," was an original production, for he wrote upon the margin the words, " Unpublishable surely," though the truth is that Burns quoted it from the D'Urfey collection. A more mischievous sort of evidence is that which is based on the contents of certain old publications, upon which the flight of time has conferred that arbitrary authority usually associated in the popular mind with "gude black prent." It is one of these whose contents and title-page we have reproduced, and which may be said to embrace the whole subject, that we propose to examine in the light of the information we have been enabled to collect. A short time before Burns's introduction to Edinburgh society, William Smellie, Lord Newton, Charles Hay, and a few more wits of the Parliament House, had founded a convivial club called "The Crochallan Fencibles" (a mock allusion to the Buonaparte Volunteer movement), which met in a tavern kept by a genial old Highlandman named "Daunie Douglas," whose favourite song, "Cro Chalien," suggested the dual designation of the Club. Smellie introduced Burns as a member in January, 1787. Cleghorn also appears to have been on the muster-roll of this rollicking regiment, which supplies a key to much of Burns's correspondence with him. How the revelry of the boon companions was stimulated and diversified may be easily imagined.

At the outset, it may be interesting to enquire as to the sources of Burns's ballad lore apart from oral tradition. With the works of Fergusson and Ramsay he was specially familiar, and his writings also testify that the English poets and dramatists were not unknown to him, but these must be adjudged indifferent aids in his researches. D'Urfey's *Pills to Purge Melancholy* was published in 1719; Ramsay's *Tea-Table Miscellany* in 1724; and William Thomson's *Orpheus Caledonius* about the same date. Previous to these, however, the *Watson Collection* was in circulation, having been published in 1709.[2] Of the last-named work. Burns says that it was "the first of its nature which has been published in our own native Scots dialect." *A Collection of Loyal Songs, Poems, &c.*, is referred to by Stenhouse as having been published in 1750, and the following year Yair's *Charmer* was issued. *The Blackbird*, edited by William Hunter, appeared in 1764; Bishop Percy's *Reliques*, 1605, the *Dublin Collection* in 1769; and Herd's *Scottish Songs*,

Heroic Ballads, &c. (referred to by Burns as *Wotherspoon's Collection*), in 1776.[3] Nearer the close of Burns's career we find *Pinkerton's Collection* in 1786; Lawrie and Symington's Collection in 1791; *Ritson's* in 1794; and *Dale's*, which Robert Chambers assigns to a period anterior to Burns without mentioning the exact date. In this list, which does not pretend to be either accurate or complete, we have disregarded such collections as Oswald's (1740), and MacGibbon's (1762), for the reason that they deal less with the poetical than the musical side of the subject. It is perhaps too much to say that Burns was conversant with the whole of these publications, but that he perused the pages of the more important of them is beyond a doubt. In the Thomson letter (Nov., 1794,) already quoted from, Burns acknowledges receipt of Ritson's work, and goes on to say:—

"Despairing of my own powers to give you variety enough in English songs, I have been turning over old collections to pick out songs of which the measure is something similar to what I want; and with a little alteration, so as to suit the rhythm of the air exactly, to give you them for your work. … You may think meanly of this one ('Dainty Davie'), but take a look of the bombast original and you will be surprised that I have made so much of it." A thoroughly satisfactory examination demands that the annotator should have before him the contents at least of these old collections. But, in the absence of reprints, those of more remote date are so extremely scarce as almost to preclude the possibility of such a method of treatment. We are, therefore, left no choice but to utilise the material at our disposal as best we may, for the purpose of demonstrating that the association of Burns's name, either as author or editor, with the ribald volumes entitled "The Merry Muses," is not only an unwarranted mendacity, but one of the grossest outrages ever perpetrated on the memory of a man of genius.

Chief amongst the assailants on the personal side of Burns is George Gilfillan, who ought to have been the last to gird at the frailties of human nature. His mental idiosyncrasies and impulsive aberrations were frequently the cause of keenest regret to his best friends. He was dogmatic and overbearing to the last degree, impatient of the opinions of others, pertinaciously obstinate in holding to first conclusions in face of the most convincing evidence of their untenability, and possessed, moreover, of the most overweening confidence in his own judgment. He was so prejudiced and pronounced in most of his estimates of men and things that one of his friends has described him as a man

"So over violent or over civil,
That every man with him was God or Devil."

In his youth he became obsessed with the idea that the latter portion of Burns's career was a continuous descent morally and physically, and he doggedly adhered to this belief to the end of his days. His opinions in 1878, when he edited *The National Burns*, are identical with those he held in 1847, when, in the 143rd number of *Hogg's Instructor*, he passed merciless judgment on Burns, based on gutter gossip of Dumfries raked together with set purpose more than half a century after the Poet had gone to his rest. He was challenged at the time by Hugh Macdonald, the well-known author of *Rambles Round Glasgow*, and an edifying newspaper controversy ensued which was afterwards published in pamphlet form, copies of which are now extremely rare.[4] With the evidence then at command, and which of course fell immeasurably short of what is now available, Macdonald so pulverised him that Gilfillan lost his temper and made matters worse by dragging into the controversy the authorship of the *Merry Muses*. To reproduce the flimsy grounds on which he sought to incriminate Burns were to repeat the original offence. The only part of the evidence submitted which is deserving of notice is his quotations from Byron's

Journal and letters. In his Journal Byron wrote:—

"Allen has lent me a quantity of Burns's unpublished, and never to be published, letters. They are full of oaths and obscene songs. What an antithetical mind! Tenderness, roughness, delicacy, coarseness, sentiment, sensuality, soaring and grovelling, dirt and deity, all mixed up in one compound of poor clay."   In a letter to Bowles he further says:—

"I have seen myself a collection of letters of another eminent—nay, pre-eminent—deceased poet, so abominably gross and elaborately coarse, that I do not believe they could be paralleled in our language. What is more strange is, that some of them are couched as postscripts to his serious and sentimental letters, to which are tacked either a piece of prose or some verses of the most hyperbolical obscenity. He himself says, 'if obscenity were the sin against the Holy Ghost, he most certainly could not be saved.'"   In another letter to his friend Hodgson, of date December 14th, 1873, he writes in similar terms:—

"Will you tell Drury I have a treasure for him—a whole set of original Burns letters never published, nor to be published; for they are full of fearful oaths[5] and the most nauseous songs— all humorous, but coarse bawdry. However they are curiosities, and shew him quite in a new point of view—the mixture, or rather contrast of tenderness, delicacy, obscenity, and coarseness in the same mind is wonderful."   These letters which seemed so "strange" to Byron—such a "treasure," such "curiosities"—were all addressed to Robert Cleghorn, farmer, Saughton Mills, who, as we have already said, was a member of the Crochallan Club, and at the same time a bosom friend of Burns. When the Poet was engaged in collecting the old songs as material for purified versions in Johnson's and Thomson's publications, whenever he came across a specially brilliant black diamond, he facetiously passed it on to Cleghorn "for his spiritual nourishment and growth in grace," and as often as not "with the Devil's blessing." These confidences were usually attached as addenda to Cleghorn's letters by way of advance copies for behoof of the rollicking company of Fencibles at their next meeting. This is the explanation of the "postscripts" which Byron could not possibly understand, and which, being set down without note or comment, led to his utter bewilderment and erroneous impression of their origin. The quotation he gives is from one of Burns's letters to Cleghorn (Oct. 25th, 1793), which, by the way, is a signal illustration of Burns himself being the leading—frequently the only—witness for his own prosecution. The "Allen" referred to by Byron was librarian to Lord Holland, and one of Byron's intimate friends. How Cleghorn's letters came to be in his possession is thus accounted for. Cleghorn married a widow named Mrs Allen, who had a son, John, by her first husband. This John Allen, of Holland House, was therefore Cleghorn's stepson, who inherited his stepfather's estate and personal effects, amongst the latter being the letters in question. The Byronic evidence consequently resolves itself into a violation of the privacy of the confidential communications which passed between Burns and Cleghorn—an eventuality never dreamed of by Burns, for he repeatedly cautioned Cleghorn and other correspondents under similar circumstances to exercise the utmost care in preserving the privacy of such communications. But all evidence of the sort is entirely beside the question of the authorship of the printed volume which so offended the susceptibilities of Gilfillan, and which, by implication, he asserted to be typed from Burns's manuscript. It need not be pointed out what a large demand this assertion makes upon our credulity in the absence of the slightest attempt at proof. Gilfillan had but scant knowledge of the subject, and his laboured effort to substitute the Cleghorn letters for the manuscript volume is a typical example of the purblind and unscrupulous methods he adopted when dealing with the character of the National Poet. Regarding this manuscript, the characteristic candour of Burns's own testimony leaves little for others to say. In a letter to John M'Murdo, of date December,

1793, occurs the following passage:—

"I think I once mentioned something of a collection of Scots songs I have for some years been making; I send you a perusal of what I have got together. I could not conveniently spare them above five or six days, and five or six glances of them will probably more than suffice you. A very few of them are my own. When you are tired of them please leave them with Mr. Clint of the King's Arms. There is not another copy of the collection in the world, and I should be sorry that any unfortunate negligence should deprive me of what has cost me a good deal of pains."

This speaks for itself, and that right eloquently. The postscript to Thomson's letter of January 20th, 1793, by the Hon. Andrew Erskine, throws such a strong sidelight on the environment of Bums and one phase of the social life of his period, as to confer upon it a special title to quotation:—

"You kindly promised me, about a year ago, a collection of your unpublished productions, *religious* and amorous. I know from experiment how irksome it is to copy. If you will get any trusty person in Dumfries to write them over fair, I will give Peter Hill whatever he asks for his trouble, and I certainly shall not betray your confidence." To this the obliging Poet replied, almost by return of post:—

"My most respectful compliments to the honourable gentleman who favoured me with a postscript in your last. He shall hear from me and receive his MSS soon." It would appear, however, that he had become aware of the peculiar tastes of this class of correspondent as early as 1787. On November 6th of that year, he writes to James Hoy, Gordon Castle, in the following terms:— "Johnson sends the books by the fly, as directed, and begs me to enclose his most grateful thanks. My return I intended should have been one or two poetic bagatelles, which the world have (*sic*) not seen, or, perhaps, for obvious reasons, cannot see. These I shall send you before I leave Edinburgh. They may make you laugh a little, which, on the whole, is the best way of spending one's precious hours and still more precious breath; at any rate they will be, though a small, yet a very sincere mark of my respectful esteem for a gentleman whose further acquaintance I should look upon as a peculiar obligation." The effusions forwarded to his boon companions of the Crochallan Club were more of the nature of replies to solicitations than voluntary offerings on his part; besides, the membership of that Club ought to be studied before the application of individual strictures. In 1793 he thus writes to Cleghorn: —

"For you I make a present of the following new edition of an old Cloaciniad song, a species of composition which I have heard you admire, and a kind of song which I knew you wanted much. It is sung to an old tune something like 'Tak' your auld cloak about ye.'" There was twa wives, and twa witty wives,
☐ Sat o'er a stoup o' brandy.

God speed the plough, and send a good seedtime. Amen! farewell!" That is the beginning and end of this "old Cloaciniad," for we can find no trace of it in any of the collections we have examined. That he did not scatter these "bagatelles," as he calls them, broadcast with careless hand, is apparent from another letter to Cleghorn, dated 21st August, 1795.[6]

"Inclosed you have Clarke's 'Gaffer Gray.' I have not time to copy it, so when you have taken a copy for yourself please return me the original. I need not caution you against giving copies to any other person. 'Peggy Ramsay' I shall expect to find in 'Gaffer Gray's' company when he returns to Dumfries." His own dispassionate opinion of these *jeux d'esprit* will be found in detached notes scattered through his correspondence, but a sufficient idea of the inner workings of his mind when the shadow of death was upon him can be gathered from his letter to Thomson of 18th May, 1796:—

"When your Publication is finished I intend publishing a collection, on a cheap plan, of all the songs I have written for you—the *Museum*, &c.—at least, of all the songs of which I wish to be called the author. I do not propose this so much in the way of emolument, as to do justice to my Muse, lest I should be blamed for trash I never saw, or be defrauded by other claimants of what is justly my own."   Two months afterwards the grave closed over him, and he left his papers, as he left himself, in naked honesty to the world, without a shred of canting deceit or unctuous pretence to conceal the flaws of that defaced image which is the common heritage of humanity. When "curst necessity" compelled him to implore the loan of five pounds, we have it on the authority of Professor Wilson that "a miscreant, aware of his poverty, made him an offer of fifty pounds for a collection"—this self-same manuscript collection—" which he repelled with horror." How, then, did it come to pass that the "horror" was re-enacted over his grave? The miserable story cannot be better told than in the unbiassed, sympathetic words of Robert Chambers:—

"Unluckily, Burns's collection of these facetiæ (including his own essays in the same walk) fell, after his death, into the hands of one of those publishers who would sacrifice the highest interests of humanity to put an additional penny into their own purses[7]; and, to the lasting grief of all the friends of our Poet, they were allowed the honours of the press. The mean-looking volume which resulted should be a warning to all honourable men of letters against the slightest connection with clandestine literature, much more the degradation of contributing to it. It may also serve as a curious study to those who take a delight in estimating the possible varieties of intellectual mood and of moral sensation of which our nature is capable,"   To this Scott Douglas adds:—[8]

"In Dumfries he carefully kept the book under lock and key; but, some years after his death, it fell into the hands of a person who caused it to be printed in a very coarse style, under the title of 'The Merry Muses of Caledonia,' post 8vo, pp. 128. The Poet's name, however, is not on the title page, nor indicated in any way except by the unmistakable power exhibited in some of the pieces."   The MS. appears to have been broken up by the "person" referred to, for what appear to be stray leaves of it still find their way occasionally into the manuscript market.

From the character of the type employed, this "mean-looking volume" must have been published *circa* 1800, but in the absence of any date on the title page the exact year can only be guessed at. Perfect copies of it are now so rare that, although fragments have repeatedly come under our observation, we have only succeeded, after years of hunting, in obtaining a sight of one complete copy.[9] It does not appear that this Dumfries volume was ever reprinted, but edition after edition of "Merry Muses" continued to be issued from the disreputable press in all parts of the kingdom, and sold privately for dishonourable gain. These, for the most part, are merely receptacles for the floating obscenity of their periods, and bear the same relation to the Dumfries edition as they do to the other sources which they laid under contribution. We have sifted no fewer than seven of these editions and reprints. On every one of the title pages appears a doggerel stanza, which will be found *in situ* in the present volume.

As the text of the original Dumfries edition is reproduced in this volume, whatever is necessary in the way of elucidation will be found in the notes appended to the individual compositions.

No. II. curtails the title to "The Merry Muses—a choice Collection of Favourite Songs;" and it bears on the lower part of the title page, "Dublin—Printed for the Booksellers—Price three shillings." There is no date. It measures 8 inches by 4½.[10]

No. III. expands the title to "The Merry Muses—a choice collection of Favourite Songs Gathered From Many Sources—by Robert Burns—to which is added Two of his letters and a poem— hitherto suppressed—and never before printed." At the top of the title page is—"Not for maids, ministers, or striplings;" and at the bottom, "Privately Printed—(Not for sale)—1827." On the reverse appears, "Only 99 copies printed." This edition has also a preface of some length. It measures 6½ inches by 4¾.

No. IV. has the same title as No. II., but bears, "Dublin—Printed for the Booksellers—1832." It measures 5⅛ inches by 3⅜.

No. V. appears to be a reprint of No. IV., and bears, "Dublin—Printed for the Booksellers—Price four shillings." There is no date. It measures 5¾ inches by 3½.

No. VI. is identical with II., IV., and V. It bears, "London—Printed for the Booksellers—1843." It measures 6½ inches by 4.

No. VII. is a reproduction of No. III., including the date, though it is evidently much more modern. It measures 7 inches by 4½.

No. VIII. is another reproduction of No. III., evidently with the date falsified.[11] On the reverse of the title page, however, is the addendum, "Only 90 copies printed," which is omitted in VII.

The copy of No. II., which fell under our observation, was, unfortunately, incomplete, 42 pp. being awanting out of a total of about 100. The new pieces are mostly of English and Irish origin, but the want of a table of contents rendered a correct list of these an impossibility. On the last page we observed a doggerel fragment on "Barm," which will be found in *Herd's Collection*. The old version of "Dainty Davie" given, is also printed in the same work in fragmentary form. An old Scots piece entitled "The Lang Dow," and a version of "For a' that and a' that," complete the list of interpolations in this edition, so far as we had opportunity of noting them. Burns's name does not appear on any part of the fragment.

No. III. is the most noteworthy edition after the Dumfries, because of its title page, on which Burns's name appears for the first time. In a somewhat lengthy and hotch-potch preface, most of which is taken from Robert Chambers without acknowledgment, the editor or compiler goes on to say:—

"This note is therefore written to point out Burns's share in this Collection of Merry Songs—a share which was chiefly that of collector, and not that of author; besides, to request of the limited number of antiquarian admirers, into whose hands the volume will find its way, that they will be careful of it, and keep it out of the way of youth, innocence, and beauty. To gratify the aforesaid antiquaries two letters of the Great Poet are now given for the first time, and also an unpublished poem from the original manuscript in Burns's own writing."   An attempt is made to separate the compositions ascribed to Burns from the others, with the result that only twelve pieces, out of a total of eighty-two, are laid to the charge of the illustrious name under cover of which the sordid wretches hoped to drive a roaring "antiquarian" trade in the literary department. The *unpublished* poem introduced with such a flourish of trumpets is "The Court of Equity," published privately in pamphlet form about 1810, and of which the version given is both inaccurate and incomplete, as we have proved by comparing it with the Egerton MSS. in the British Museum. We have seen another version as an appendix to an Alnwick edition of Burns, published about the same date; a third will be found in the Aldine edition of 1893; while a fourth, for private circulation, was published in Glasgow about half-a-dozen years ago. An edition, "printed for the author," was published in Edinburgh in 1910. The majority of these are either garbled or incomplete. The letters are confidential communications, shamelessly filched from private repositories. One of them addressed to James Johnson, from Mauchline, 25th May, 1788, will be found in Paterson's Scott Douglas (Vol. v., p. 125), and also in Hately Waddell's edition (Special Correspondence, p. 79); the other has never been published under respectable auspices. Of the eighty-two pieces printed, no fewer than forty-two do not appear in the Dumfries edition; yet upon the fly title-page is printed the libel, "Burns's Merry Muses." And, further, to the unconscious discredit of the whole of his "antiquarian" discoveries, the anonymous scribbler confides, with charming simplicity, his utter ignorance of the subject by appending, at the conclusion of his laudable labours, the oracular remark:—"The foregoing completes the Merry Muses as originally collected by Burns." The glozing hypocrisy of the whole performance reaches a climax, when, after submitting the old version of "John Anderson, my Jo," our penny-a-liner quotes two stanzas of Burns's version, and then eructates the following cant:—

"Where, in the English language, is there so pure and lovable a picture of happy wedded life? Reader, when you now know out of what mire the poet of Scotland had to pick up many of his best and purest lyrics, bless his memory that the legacy he left to the world was so rich, and pure, and precious." The interpolated pieces in this edition are:—[12]

Parody on "Shepherds I have lost my love."
A Sentimental Sprig.
Botany Bay.
Burlesque on "The Highland Laddie."
Burlesque on "Stella."
Cupid's Frolic.
Darby's Key.
Fanny's black jock.
Green leaves on the Green, Oh!
Jack of all Trades.
John Anderson, my jo. (Burns's version).
Langolee.
Court of Equity.
Lucy and Kitty's black jocks.
Lullaby.
My Angel, I will Marry thee.
Parody on "Corn Rigs."
Roger and Molly.
The Bonniest Lass.
The Bottle.
The Brown —— of Old England.
The Bumper Toast.
The Citadel.
The Goldfinch's Nest.
The grey jock.
The Happy Bunter.
The Highland Laddie.
The Irish Root.
The Little Tenement.
The Mouse's Tail.

The Origin of the pox.
The Pious Parson.
The Plenipotentiary.
The Reels of Bogie.
The Ride to London.
The Tailor.
The Vigorous Courtezan.
The Wishes.
Toasts and Sentiments.
Una's Lock.
Letter to Robert Ainslie (Mauchline, March 3, 1788).
Letter to James Johnson.

It may be added that of the twelve songs ascribed to Burns four are to be found in his published works, and five are docketed "perhaps by Burns, but doubtful." When we find this generous guess hazarded on such a well-authenticated old production as "An'ra, and his cutty gun," we are justified in the conclusion that the compilation is mere guess work from beginning to end. Taken at the worst, it must be matter of congratulation, coming from such a quarter, that the sum total credited to Burns is set down at three songs net, out of seventy-eight—rather a slender pretext for hoisting such a sky-cleaving signboard.

No. IV. calls for no remark beyond the table of contents, which includes twenty-six additions whose origin is unmistakably revealed in their titles:—

The Dispute.
Parody on "Sweet's the love."
The British Fair.
Fair lady lay.
Gulliver in Lilliput.
Blue Bells of Ireland.
Paudieen O'RafEerty.
The Friar.
They all do it.
Would? you do it?
Sheila-na-Guiry.
Father Paul.
Patrick Quimes.
Hall and Doll.
The Parson and Clerk.
Burlesque on the "Fair Thief."
The Wedding Night.
Comical Jack.
A Tender Young Maid.
The Double Blessing.
Amoret and Phillida.
Coxheath.
A new way to pardon Sins.
The Marriage Morn.
The End.

A Sweet Young Maid.

In No. V. appears "The tailor cam' tae clout the claes," which appears in *Herd's Collection*, 1776. It is also given in No. III.

No. VI. closely follows V., but contains three additional pieces:—

The Gipsy Girl.
Here's a Bumper to her.
Fanny is the Girl for me.

On every page is printed "Burns's Merry Muses," which entitles it to the distinguished honour of being the most villainous edition that has ever appeared.

The other volumes, being reprints pure and simple, need not be dwelt upon. Though our list is probably far from being complete, sufficient data will be found in the foregoing for an estimate of the amount of "trash he never saw," which has been foisted on the name of Burns in the interests of a nefarious trade, which is quite on a level with violating his grave and suspending his bones on the gibbet.

Returning to the Dumfries edition, and deducting double titles, we have in reality 85 individual compositions. Of these, no reprint or subsequent edition which we have examined contains more than forty, a fact which effectually disposes of any pretensions they may have to be placed on the same plane with the volume which is assumed to represent the original manuscript. Proceeding to analyse the table of contents we find, firstly, that *fifteen* of the compositions appear in one or other of the published editions of the Poet's works; the more rare, in the Kilmarnock edition of Scott Douglas. Though more or less amended in word or phrase, these still retain sufficient of their original character upon which to found a judgment. Upon the remaining seventy it would be rash to give an *ex cathedra* deliverance till a complete collection of the old works, formerly referred to, supplies whatever recoverable data may be a wanting.[13] In Burns's last interview with Maria Riddel, Professor Wilson says:—

"He expressed deep contrition for having been betrayed by his inferior nature and sympathy with the dissolute, into impurities in verse, which he knew were floating about among people of loose lives, and might, on his death, be collected to the hurt of his moral character. Never had Burns been 'hired minstrel of voluptuous blandishment,' nor by such unguarded freedom of speech had he ever sought to corrupt, but in emulating the ribald wit and coarse humour of some of the worst old ballads current among the lower orders of the people, of whom the moral and religious are often tolerant of indecencies to a strange degree, he felt he had sinned against his genius." He has been more sinned against than sinning. The testimony of such a man as Robert Burns, on anything affecting himself, is worth a whole library of conjecture. With him the unpardonable sin was the sin of lying; therefore let the truth be spoken as the best means of rebutting the falsehoods and misrepresentations which, like fungus growths, have gathered round the musty nastiness of the publications we have pilloried. Scott Douglas (Paterson's Ed., Vol. V., p. 310) makes mention of "a lot of Pickering MSS. doubtless yet in existence," from which it may be inferred that he did not peruse them; we are therefore left to guess on what authority he ascribes "The Trogger" to Burns, a stanza of which he quotes in the same edition (Vol. III., p. 247). In the Kilmarnock Edition (Vol. II., p. 417) he plainly informs his readers that he never saw these MSS., but that Mr. Greenshields of Kerse, Lesmahago, had "kindly favoured him with transcripts of some, and interesting information regarding others." On 9th June, 1871, the same gentleman (he goes on to say) wrote to him in the following terms:—"On broad moral ground, I have just finished a bonfire of them—so here ends the matter." It is therefore a certainty that the

Greenshields part of the Pickering collection is beyond recovery. "The Jolly Gauger"—an amended version of which is given at p. 422 of Vol. II. of same edition, taken along with the note attached—is a warning of the danger of allowing such commendable qualities as editorial conscientiousness and enthusiasm to run riot. In Vol. II. (pp. 60 and 62, Paterson's Ed.) reference is made to other two "Crochallan" songs—"The bonie Moor Hen," and "My Lord a-Hunting"— the former of which is mentioned in the Clarinda correspondence. What are we then to understand by "Crochallan" songs as distinguished from songs in the "Crochallan" collection? Was the "mean-looking volume" a faithful reflection of the pilfered MS., or was it, like its successors, composed of garbled extracts eked out by the canticular obscenity of its time? We cannot say, and we submit its contents with that reservation. From his tomb comes the lingering echo, "a very few of them are my own." What more is there in that confession than half the world, were it only half as honest, could confess of the "original sin" of bachelor stories in bachelor clubs, the modern demand for prurient novels, and the insatiable curiosity that centres in the proceedings of the Divorce Courts? Were the private confidences of either the celebrated or obscure of any age or time as ruthlessly violated as those of Burns have been, few would escape whipping. Our purpose will have been served if this publication be the means of furnishing the Poet's admirers with a sufficiency of fact wherewith to repel the calumnies and falsehoods which the cupidity of a few infamous publishers has heaped upon his name.

Wordsworth, the poet, who in 1816 perused a printed copy of the "Merry Muses" (very likely the Dumfries edition), expressed his opinion of its reputed authorship in the following words:—[14]

"He must be a miserable judge of poetical compositions who can for a moment fancy that such low, tame, and loathsome ribaldry can possibly be the production of Burns. With the utmost difficulty we procured a slight perusal of the abominable pamphlet alluded to. The truth is (and we speak on the best authority the country can produce), there is not one verse in that miscellany that ever was publicly acknowledged by Burns, nor is there above a single page that can be traced to his manuscript."   On the subject, Henley says:—

"He was made welcome (in Edinburgh) by the ribald, scholarly, hard-drinking wits and jinkers of the Crochallan Fencibles, for whose use and edification he made the unique and precious collection now called the 'Merry Muses of Caledonia.' "   This is surprisingly just but scarcely correct. The first purpose of the "collection" was for Burns's own use when providing purified versions of the old songs for Johnson and Thomson. What the same authority says of the Ainslie letter of March 3rd, 1788, cannot be passed over without comment:—

"The original," says Henley, "must be read, or the reader will never wholly understand what manner of man the writer was."   We say at once that such a letter should not have been preserved by any friend of Burns, far less by an intimate friend like Ainslie. But the covert inference is neutralised in great degree by the undisputable fact that Burns was married to Jean Armour two years prior to the date of the letter. The burning of the "marriage lines" did not annul the "irregular marriage" for which Burns and Jean Armour were reproved by the Kirk Session of Mauchline in 1788, and taken bound to adhere to each other during their natural lives. When Mr. Auld granted Bums a certificate as a bachelor he did so in ignorance of the private marriage which had taken place previous to the appearance of both before the Kirk Session for discipline as unmarried persons. The Ainslie letter bears on the face of it that it was a bachelor communication to a trusted bachelor friend who had a *penchant* for facetiae of the sort; and Burns never did things by halves. It has never been published under respectable auspices. Ainslie's gross breach of confidence in preserving this letter contrasts strangely with Burns's tender handling of the former's *faux pas* with the cottar's daughter at Dunse.[15] Whatever he may have been in his earlier years, Robert Ainslie does not appear to advantage in his correspondence with Cromek, when the latter was collecting material for his "Reliques." That he was a friend of the fair-weather species appears from a letter of Burns to Clarinda, dated June 25th, 1794, in which he says:—

"I had a letter from him (Ainslie) a while ago, but it was so dry, so distant, so like a card to one of his clients, that I could scarce bear to read it, and have not yet answered it. He is a good, honest fellow, and can write a friendly letter. . . . Though Fame does not blow her trumpet at my approach now, as she did then, when he first favoured me with his friendship, yet I am as proud as ever; and when I am laid in my grave, I wish to be stretched at my full length, that I may occupy every inch of ground I have a right to."   The tombstones of Burns's contemporaries are in the valley; his is set upon an hill and cannot be hid.

In treating of the text, no attempt has been made to trace the authorship of the various compositions save by the evidence contained in the notes. We do not believe in the infallibility of any man's Burns instinct, nor can any just judgment be based on the shifting sand of "the power exhibited in some of the pieces." Neither can any of the compositions be rightly ascribed to Burns for the sole reason that they cannot be traced further back than his period. He dug in fallow ground and filled his notebook for the most part from oral recital of what had passed from ear to ear during many generations. We therefore leave the reader to draw his own conclusions with regard to the extent of Burns's contributions to the "clandestine literature" which is here reprinted as it appeared in the "mean-looking volume" published in Dumfries a few years after his death. Whether or not the dishonourable miscreant who purloined the Poet's manuscript collection from his over-confiding widow, adhered strictly to the text, or corrupted and added to it like his enterprising successors, is a question which cannot now be answered with certainty.

In conclusion, we may thus summarise the discussion:

I. It may be held proved that Burns formed a collection of old Scots songs of a ribald nature for his own use and the amusement of the Crochallan Club.

II. He was aware of its value as a historical and literary curiosity, and treasured it as similar records have been preserved in all languages; yet he was keenly alive to the necessity of keeping it from the gaze of the merely curious and prurient-minded.

III. That the MS. was filched from his wife on false pretences after his decease, and never returned.

IV. That it was printed, probably in Dumfries, *circa* 1800, and a limited number put in circulation.

V. Presuming that it was a faithful reproduction of the MS., it contains 85 compositions in verse. Burns's name appears nowhere in the book, the title of which is:—"The Merry Muses of Caledonia—A Collection of Favourite Scots Songs (ancient and modem)—Selected for the use of the Crochallan Fencibles."

VI. Of these 85 compositions, only 40 appeared in any subsequent reprint, nor did any subsequent reprint pretend to be in any way connected with the first or "Crochallan" edition.

VII. That a collection of obscene songs was printed in Dublin prior to 1827, bearing the title, "Merry Muses," without any reference whatever to Burns.

VIII. That in 1827, a similar collection, with 42 additional pieces, was "privately printed" somewhere. On the title page we read:—"The Merry Muses—a choice Collection of Favourite Songs gathered from many sources—by Robert Burns—to which is (sic) added two of his letters and a poem—hitherto suppressed—and never before printed." One of the letters is dated March

3rd, 1788, and is addressed, from Mauchline, to Robert Ainslie; the other, dated May 25th, 1788, and addressed to James Johnson, will be found in any standard edition of the Poet's works.

We trust the intention of the present work has now been made sufficiently clear.

VINDEX.

↑ From Cloacina, a Roman goddess, who presided over the *Cloacae* or public receptacles for the filth of the city.

↑ *Choice Drollery: Songs and Sonnets*, was published in 1656; *Westminster Drolleries*, in 1672; and *Merry Drollery*, in 1691. These are more closely connected with English literature.

↑ A First Edition.

↑ For reprint of same see *Burns Chronicle* (No. IV., 1895).

↑ Byron here draws on his imagination; none of the MSS bear this out.

↑ See also "Edinburgh Commonplace Book," 1787.

↑ It was obtained on loan from Mrs. Burns on false pretences, and never returned.

↑ Paterson's Ed., Vol. ii. p. 47. See also Kilmarnock Ed. Preface, p. xlviii.

↑ The copy referred to is the only complete copy of the original edition known to exist, and was at one time the property of Mr. W. Scott Douglas, as the manuscript notes in his hand testify.

↑ The measurements apply to the copies examined.

↑ The copy in our possession, judging from the type, binding, and spotless condition, has certainly been printed within the last dozen years or so.

↑ Indelicate titles have been altered or amended.

↑ See Kilmarnock Edition, Vol. II., p. 343.

↑ Lockhart's Life of Burns—Appendix; London: Geo. Bell & Sons; 1892.

↑ See "Robin shure in hairst."

THE FORNICATOR.
Tune—"*Clout the Cauldron.*"

This is an early production of Burns, and refers to the public rebuke administered to him by the Kirk Session, in the Autumn of 1784, following on the birth of "his dear-bought Bess," whose mother was Elizabeth Paton, a servant of the family while in Lochlea. An altered version will be found in Scott Douglas's Kilmarnock edition (vol. ii., p. 420). Burns usually draws upon his imagination when writing in this vein. The "roguish boy," for instance, was of the opposite sex in reality.

Ye jovial boys, who love the joys,
　The blissful joys of lovers,
And dare avow wi' dauntless brow,
　Whate'er the lass discovers;
I pray draw near, and you shall hear,
　And welcome in a frater,
I've lately been in quarantine,
　A proven fornicator.

Before the congregation wide
　I pass'd the muster fairly,
My handsome Betsy by my side,
　We gat our ditty rarely.
My downcast eye, by chance did spy
　What made my mouth to water,
[1]Those hills of snow which wyled me so,
　To be a fornicator.

Wi' ruefu' face, and signs o' grace,
　I paid the buttock hire;
The night was dark, and thro' the park,
　I couldna but convoy her.
A parting kiss, what could I less;
　My vows began to scatter,
Sweet Betsy fell, fal, lal, de ral.
　And I'm a fornicator.

But by the sun and moon I swear,
　And I'll fulfill ilk hair o't,
That while I own a single crown,
　She's welcome to a share o't.
My roguish boy, his mother's joy.
　And darling of his pater,

I for his sake, the name will take,
☐A hardened fornicator.

↑ or, Those limbs so clean, where I between,
Commenced a fornicator.

BEWARE OF THE RIPPLES.
Tune—"*The Tailer fell thro' the bed*."

This is an old song, on which Burns modelled "The Bonie Moor-Hen," which Clarinda advised him not to publish "for your sake, and for mine," in a letter dated January 30, 1788. Scott Douglas published it in his Kilmarnock edition, with a quotation from the old version in his introductory note (Vol. II., p. 275).

I rede you beware o' the ripples, young man,
I rede you beware o' the ripples, young man,
Tho' the saddle be saft, ye needna ride aft,
For fear that the girdin' beguile you, young man.

I rede you beware o' the ripples, young man,
I rede you beware o' the ripples, young man;
Tho' music be pleasure, tak' music in measure,
Or ye may want wind in your whistle, young man.

I rede you beware o' the ripples, young man,
I rede you beware o' the ripples, young man;
Whate'er you bestow, do less than ye dow,
The mair will be thought of your kindness, young man.

I rede you beware o' the ripples, young man,
I rede you beware o' the ripples, young man,
If you would be strang, and wish to live lang.
Dance less wi' your a—e to the kipples, young man.

THE LASS O' LIVISTON.

Burns mentions this song in the samples of old pieces surviving among the peasentry of the West of Scotland which he sent to Lord Woodhouselee, in August 1787. Cromek garbled Burns's note on the song (as was his wont) in his "Select Scottish Songs," published in 1810. James C. Dick gives the correct note in his "Notes on Scottish Song by Robert Burns," published in 1908. It is as follows:— "'Pain'd with her slighting Jamie's love,
Bell dropt a tear—Bell dropt a tear;
The gods descended from above
Well pleased to hear, well pleased to hear,' &c. The original set of verses to this tune is still extant, and have a very great deal of poetic merit, but are not quite ladies' reading." The stanza quoted is from an old song of decorous character.   The bonnie lass o' Liviston,
Her name ye ken, her name ye ken,
And aye the welcomer you'll be.
The farther ben, the farther ben.
And she has written in her contract,
To lie her lane, to lie her lane;
And I have written in my contract.
To claw her wame, to claw her wame.

The bonny lass o' Liviston,
She's berry brown, she's berry brown;
And ye winna trow her raven locks,
Gae farther down, gae farther down.
She has a black and rolling e'e.
And a dimplit chin, a dimplit chin,
And no to prie her bonnie mou'
Wad be a sin, wad be a sin.

The bonnie lass o' Liviston,
Came in to me, came in to me,
I wat wi' baith ends o' the busk,
I made her free, I made her free;
I laid her feet to my bed-stock.
Her head to the wa', her head to the wa',
And I gied her her wee coat in her teeth,
Her sark and a', her sark and a'.

SHE'S HOY'D ME OUT O' LAUDERDALE.

An old song recovered by Burns. He incorporated the fifth line of the last stanza in "The Deuks Dang o'er my Daddie, O!" An amended version will be found in the Aldyne edition of 1893.

There liv'd a lady in Lauderdale,
　She lo'ed a fiddler fine;
She lo'ed him in her chamber,
　She held him in her mind;
She made his bed at her bed-stock.
　She said he was her brither;
But she's hoy'd him out o' Lauderdale,
　His fiddle and a' thegither.

First when I cam' to Lauderdale,
　I had a fiddle gude.
My sounding-pin stood lie the aik
　That grows in Lauder wood;
But now my sounding-pin's gaen down,
And tint the foot for ever;
She's hoy'd me out o' Lauderdale,
　My fiddle and a' thegither.

First when I cam' to Lauderdale,
　Your ladyship can declare,
I play'd a bow, a noble bow.
　As e'er was strung wi' hair:
But dow'na do's come o'er me now.
　And your ladyship winna consider;
She's hoy'd me out o' Lauderdale,
　My fiddle and a' thegither.

Tune—"*The dearest o' the Quorum.*"

The heroine of this song was Ann Park, a niece of Mrs. Hyslop, of the Globe Tavern, Dumfries, and mother of Burns's illegitimate daughter Elizabeth, who was brought up by Jean Armour as one of her own children. She was born March 31st, 1791; was married to John Thomson, Pollokshaws, to whom she bore a large family; and died at Crossmyloof, June, 1873, aged 82. The Globe Tavern was where Burns lodged when his Excise duties precluded his return to Ellisland, and it remained to the end of his days his favourite "howff "in Dumfries. What became of "Anna" is not certainly known. Burns had an extravagant notion of the merits of this song. He copied the first two double stanzas into the Glenriddell MS. collection, and the third stanza appears on another page of the same book. The "postscript" was added for the benefit of the "Crochallan Fencibles." He sent a colder-toned version to Thomson, who did not consider it suitable for his "Collection." In the accompanying letter Burns writes—"'The Banks of Banna" is to me a heavenly air—what would you think of a set of Scots verses to it? I made one a good while ago, which I think is the best love song I ever composed in my life; but in its original state it is not quite a lady's song." This song is printed in Scott Douglas's Edinburgh edition exactly as it appears here (Vol. II., p. 292). A MS. of this song, in Burns's hand, was sold at the Hoe sale, New York, in May, 1911.

Yestre'en I had a pint o' wine,
☐A place where body saw na,
 Yestre'en lay on this breast o' mine,
☐The gowden locks o' Anna.
 The hungry Jew in wilderness,
☐Rejoicing o'er his manna,
 Was naething to my hiney bliss.
☐Upon the lips of Anna.

 Ye Monarchs, take the East and West,
☐Frae Indus to Savannah;
 Gi'e me within my straining grasp,
☐The melting form o' Anna.
 Then I'll despise imperial charms,
☐An Empress or Sultana,
 While dying raptures in her arms
☐I give and take wi' Anna.

 Awa', thou flaunting God o' Day,
☐Awa', thou pale Diana,
 Ilk star gae hide thy twinkling ray
☐When I'm to meet my Anna.
 Come in thy raven plumage, Night,
☐Sun, moon, and stars withdrawn a'.
 And bring an angel pen to write
☐My raptures wi' my Anna.

POSTSCRIPT BY ANOTHER HAND.

The Kirk and State may join and tell
 To do sic things I maunna,
The Kirk and State may gae to h—l,
 And I'll gae to my Anna.
She is the sunshine o' my e'e,
 To love but her I canna;
Had I on earth but wishes three,
 The first should be my Anna.

ERROCK BRAE.

Tune—*"Sir Alex. Don's Strathspey."*

This is an old song current among the peasantry of that day.

O Errock stane, may never maid
  A maiden by thee gae,
Nor e'er a stan' o' stan'in' graith,
  Gae stannin' o'er the brae.

  For tillin' Errock brae, young man,
  And tillin' Errock brae,
  An open fur, and stan'in' graith,
  Maun till the Errock brae.

As I sat by the Errock stane,
  Surveying far and near.
Up came a Cameronian,
  Wi' a' his preaching gear.

  For tillin', etc.

He flang the Bible o'er the brae,
  Amang the rashy gerse,
But the Solemn League and Covenant,
  He laid below my a—e.

  For tillin', etc.

But on the edge of Errock brae,
  He gae me sic a sten.
That o'er, and o'er, and o'er we row'd,
  Till we cam' to the glen.

  For tillin', etc.

Yet still his p—t—e held the grip,
  And still his b—l—ks hang,
That a Synod couldna tell the a—e,
  To wham they did belang.

  For tillin', etc.

    A Prelate he loups on before,
  A Catholic behin',

But gi'e me a Cameronian,
He f——s a body blin'.

For tillin'. etc.

MY AUNTIE JEAN.
Tune—"*John Anderson, my jo.*"

This fragment is attributed to Burns. In a letter to Samuel Brown, Ballochneil, Kirkoswald (his mother's half-brother), dated May, 1788, he refers to the "Ailsa fowling season," and asks him to procure for him "three or four stones of feathers."

My auntie Jean held to the shore,
☐As Ailsa boats cam' back;
And she has coft a feather bed
☐For twenty and a plack;
And in it she wan fifty mark,
☐Before a towmond sped;
O! what a noble bargain
☐Was auntie Jeanie's bed.

OUR GUDEWIFE'S SAE MODEST.
Tune—"*John Anderson, my jo.*"
This is an old fragment.

Our gudewife's sae modest.
When she is set at meat,
A laverock's leg, or a tittling's wing,
Is mair than she can eat;
But, when she's in her bed at e'en,
Between me and the wa';
She is a glutton deevil.
She swallows c—ds and a'.

WAD YE DO THAT?
Tune—"*John Anderson, my jo.*"
An old song before Burns' s time.

Gudewife, when your gudeman's frae hame,
Might I but be sae bauld,
As come into your bed-chamber,
When winter nights are cauld?
As come into your bed-chamber,
When nights are cauld and wat,
And lie down in your gudeman's stead,
Gudewife, wad ye do that?

Young man, if ye should be so kind,
When my gudeman's frae hame,
As come into my bed-chamber.
Where I am laid my lane.
And lie down in my gudeman's stead,
Young man, I'll tell you what,
He f——s me five times ilka night.
Young man, wad ye do that?

A' THAT AND A' THAT.

The refrain is an old one, common to several old songs of this kind. Burns followed the old model in the "bard's song" of the "Jolly Beggars," as well as in his immortal ode "A man's a man for a' that."

Put butter in my Donald's brose,
  For weel does Donald fa' that;
I lo'e my Donald's tartan hose,
  His naked a—e, and a' that.

  For a' that and a' that.
  And twice as mickle's a' that,
  The lassie gat a skelpit doup,
  But wan the day for a' that.

For Donald swore a solemn aith,
  By his first hairy gravat,
That he would fecht the battle there,
  And stick the lass and a' that.

  For a' that, etc.

His hairy b—l—ks side and wide,
  Hung like a beggar's wallet;
His p—k stood like a rollin' pin.
  She nicher'd when she saw that.

  For a' that, etc.

Then she turned up her h—ry c—t,
  And she bade Donald claw that;
The devil's dizzen Donald drew,
  And Donald gied her a' that.

  For a' that, etc.

MUIRLAND MEG.
Tune—"*Eppy Macnab.*"
An old song, a copy of which exists in Burns's handwriting.

Amang our young lasses there's Muirland Meg,
She'll beg or she work, and she'll play or she beg;
At thretteen her maidenhead flew to the gate,
An' the door o' her cage stands open yet.

☐And for a sheep-cloot she'll do't, she'll do't,
☐And for a sheep-cloot she'll do't;
☐And for a toop-horn she'll do't to the morn,
☐And merrily turn and do't, and do't.

Her kittle black een they wad thirl ye thro',
Her rosebud lips cry kiss me just now;
The curls and links o' her bonny black hair,
Wad put you in mind that the lassie has mair.

And for, etc.☐

An armfu' o' love is her bosom sae plump;
A span o' delight is her middle sae jimp,
A taper white leg, and a thumpin' thie.
And a fiddle near by ye can play a wee.

And for, etc.☐

Love's her delight and kissing's her treasure.
She'll stick at nae price an ye gie her good measure;
As lang's a sheep-fit an' as girt's a goose egg,
O, that's the measure o' Muirland Meg.

And for, etc.☐

YE HAE LIEN WRANG, LASSIE.
Tune—"*Up and waur them a', Willie.*"

An old song in circulation before Burns's day. A version of this song, almost identical with this, will be found in the Aldyne edition of 1893.

Ye hae lien wrang, lassie,
Ye hae lien a' wrang,
Ye've lien in some unco bed,
And wi' some unco man.

Your rosy cheeks are turn'd sae wan,
You're greener than the grass, lassie,
Your coatie's shorter by a span.
Yet deil an inch the less, lassie.

Ye hae lien, &c.

You've let the pownie o'er the dyke,
And he's been in the corn, lassie;
For aye the brose ye sup at e'en,
Ye bock them ere the morn, lassie.

Ye hae Hen, &c.

Fu' lightly lap ye o'er the knowe.
And thro' the wood ye sang, lassie;
But herryin' o' the foggy byke,
I fear ye've got a stang, lassie.

Ye hae lien, &c.

THE PATRIARCH.
Tune—"*The Auld Cripple Dow:*"

This is by Burns. The original MS. was in the possession of a gentleman in Forfar. It is headed—
  "A Wicked Song.
  "Author's name unknown.
  "Tune—The waukin' o' a winter's night.
  "The Publisher to the Reader,
  "Courteous Reader,
  "The following is certainly the production of one of those licentious, ungodly (too-much-abounding in this our day) wretches who take it as a compliment to be called wicked, provided you allow them to be witty. Pity it is that while so many tar barrels in the country are empty, and so many gibbets untenanted, some example is not made of these profligates." Burns pursues this satirical-humorous vein in his mock manifesto as "Poet Laureat and Bard-in-Chief of Kyle, Cuningham, and Carrick," addressed (November 20th, 1786) to William Chalmers and John M'Adam, "students and practitioners in the ancient and mysterious Science of confounding Right and Wrong." A reprint of the whole manifesto will be found in Scott Douglas's Edinburgh edition (Vol. IV., p. 163). The following extract indicates the drift of it:—
  "Be it known, that . . . we have discovered a certain nefarious, abominable, and wicked song or ballad, a copy whereof we have enclosed; Our will therefore is . . . that the said copy shall be consumed by fire at the Cross of Ayr . . . in the presence of all beholders, in abhorrence of, and terrorem to, all such compositions and composers. Given at Mauchline this twentieth day of November, Anno Domini one thousand seven hundred and eighty-six.—God Save the Bard."

  As honest Jacob on a night,
  With his beloved beauty,
Was duly laid on wedlock's bed,
  And noddin' at his duty.

Chorus—Fal de dal, &c.

  "How lang," she cried, "ye fumbling wretch,
  Will ye be f——ing at it?
My auldest wean might die o' age,
  Before that ye could get it.

Fal de dal, &c.

  "Ye pegh and grane, and goazle there,
  And make an unco splutter,
And I maun lie and thole you, though
  I'm fient a hair the better."

Fal de dal, &c.

Then he in wrath put up his graith,
☐"The devil's in the hizzie,
I mow you as I mow the lave,
☐And night and day I'm busy.

Fal de dal, &c.

"I've bairned the servant gipsies baith,
☐Forbye your titty Leah,
Ye barren jade, ye put me mad,
☐What mair can I do wi' you?

Fal de dal, &c.

"There's ne'er a mow I've gien the lave,
☐But ye hae got a dizzen.
But d——d a ane ye'se get again,
Although your c——t should gizzen."

Fal de dal, &c.

Then Rachel, calm as ony lamb,
☐She claps him on the waulies;
Quo' she, "Ne'er fash a woman's' clash,
☐In troth ye mow me brawlies.

Fal de dal, &c.

"My dear 'tis true, for mony a mow,
☐I am your gratefu' debtor,
But ance again, I dinna ken,
☐Will aiblins happen better."

Fal de dal, &c.

The honest man wi' little wark,
He soon forgot his ire;
The patriarch he coost the sark,
And up and till't like fire.

Fal de dal, &c.

CAN YE NO LET ME BE?
Tune—"*I hae laid a Herring in Saut.*"
An old song in metre characteristic of old compositions of the kind.

There lived a wife in Whistle Cockpen,
Will ye no, can ye no, let me be,
She brewed good ale for gentlemen,
And aye she waggit it wantonly.

The night blew sair wi' wind and weet,
Will ye no, can ye no, let me be?
She shewed the traveller ben to sleep,
And aye she waggit it wantonly.

She saw a sight below his sark.
Will ye no, can ye no, let me be?
She wished she had it for a merk,
And aye she waggit it wantonly.

She saw a sight aboon his knee,
Will ye no, can ye no, let me be?
She would not wanted it for three.
And aye she waggit it wantonly.

O where live ye, and what's yer trade?
Will ye no, can ye no, let me be?
I am a thresher gude, he said.
And aye she waggit it wantonly.

And that's my flail, and working graith.
Will ye no, can ye no, let me be?
And noble tools, quoth she, by my faith!
And aye she waggit it wantonly.

I would gie ye a browst, the best I hae,
Will ye no, can ye no, let me be?
For a good night's work with tools like thae,
And aye she waggit it wantonly.

I would sell the hair frae aff my tail,
Will ye no, can ye no, let me be?
To buy our Andrew sic a flail,
And aye she waggit it wantonly.

THE CASE OF CONSCIENCE.
Tune—"*Auld Sir Simon the King.*"
An old song.

    I'll tell you a tale of a wife,
☐And she was a Whig and a saunt.
  She lived a most sanctify'd life,
☐But whiles she was fashed wi' her c—t.

  Poor woman, she gaed to the Priest,
☐And to him she made her complaint,
  There's naething that troubles my breast
☐Sae sair as the sins of my c—t.

  He bade her to cheer up her brow,
☐And no be discourag'd upon't,
  For holy good women enow
☐Are mony times waur'd wi' their c—t.

  It's nocht but Beelzebub's art,
☐And that's the mair sign of a saunt,
  He kens that ye' re pure at the heart,
☐So he levels his dart at your c—t.

  O ye that are calléd and free,
☐Elected and chosen a saunt,
  Won't break the eternal decree,
☐Whatever you do wi' your c—t.

  And now wi' a sanctify'd kiss,
☐Let's kneel and renew the cov'nant.
  It's this—and it's this—and it's this,
☐That settles the pride of your c—t.

  Devotion flew up to a flame,
☐No words can do justice upon't.
  The honest auld woman gaed hame,
☐Rejoicing, and clawing her c—t.

THE TROGGER.
Tune—"*Gillicrankie.*"

Anonymous; probably not older than Burns's time. Scott Douglas quotes a stanza of it in his 6 vol. edition (Vol. III., p. 247), and gives his opinion on the authorship of the song.   As I cam' down by Annan side,
　Intending for the Border,
　Amang the Scroggie banks and braes,
　Wha met I but a trogger.
　He laid me down upon my back,
　I thought he was but jokin',
　Till he was in me to the hilts,
　the deevil tak' sic troggin!

What could I say, what could I do,
　bann'd and sair misca'd him,
But whiltie-whaltie gaed his a—e
　The mair that I forbade him;
He stell'd his foot against a stane,
　And doubl'd ilka stroke in,
Till I gaed daft amang his hands,
　O the deevil tak' sic troggin!

Then up we raise, and took the road,
　And in by Ecclefechan,
Where the brandy-stoup we gart it clink,
　And the strang-beer ream the quech in.
Bedown the bents o' Bonshaw braes,
　We took the partin' yokin';
But I've clawed a sairy c—t sin' syne,
　O the deevil tak' sic troggin!

THE REEL O' STUMPIE.
An old fragment.

Wap and rowe, wap and rowe,
Wap and rowe the feetie o't;
I thought I was a maiden fair,
Till I heard the greetie o't.

My daddie was a fiddler fine,
My minnie she made mantie, O;
And I mysel' a thumpin' quine,
And danced the reel o' stumpie, O.

GODLY GIRZIE.
Tune—"*Wat ye wha I met yestreen.*"

Anonymous, but quite in Burns's style. Burns never once mentions the Craigie hills, familiar as he was with the Kilmarnock district.

The night it was a haly night,
The day had been a haly day;
Kilmarnock gleamed wi' candle light,
As Girzie hameward took her way.
A man o' sin, ill may he thrive!
And never haly-meeting see!
Wi' godly Girzie met belyve,
Amang the Craigie hills sae hie.

The chiel was wight, the chiel was stark,
He wadna wait to chap nor ca'.
And she was faint wi' haly wark.
She had na pith to say him na.
But ay she glowr'd up to the moon,
And ay she sighed most piouslie,
"I trust my heart's in heaven aboon,
Whare'er your sinfu' p—t—e be."

GREEN GROW THE RASHES.

Regarding the ribald version of this song current in his day, Burns writes to Thomson, in April, 1793—"At any rate, my other song, 'Green grow the rashes,' will never suit. The song is current in Scotland under the old title, and to the merry old tune of that name, which of course would mar the progress of your song to celebrity. Your book will be the standard of Scots song for the future; let this idea ever keep your judgment on the alarm." From the older version in Herd's publication (1776), Burns quotes the first stanza, in a letter to John Richmond (Sept. 30, 1786), the occasion being the birth of the first twins by Jean Armour.   Green grow the rashes, O,

Green grow the rashes, O,
The lassies they hae wimble-bores,
The widows they hae gashes, O.

O wat ye ought o' fisher Meg,
And how she trow'd the wabster, O,
She loot me see her carrot c—t,
And sell'd it for a labster, O.

Green grow, &c.

Mistress Mary cow'd her thing,
Because she wad be gentle, O,
And span the fleece upon a rock.
To waft a Highland mantle, O.

Green grow, &c.

An' heard ye o' the coat o' arms
The Lyon brought our lady, O,
The crest was couchant, sable c— t,
The motto, " Ready, Ready," O.

Green grow, &c.

An' ken ye Leezie Lundie, O,
The godly Leezie Lundie, O;
She m—s like reek thro' a' the week,
But finger fr—gs on Sunday, O.

Green grow, &c.

An Older Version.

Green grow the rashes, O,
Green grow the rashes, O;
The sweetest bed that e'er I got,
Was the bellies o' the lassies, O.

'Twas late yestreen I met wi' ane
And wow but she was gentle, O;
Ae han' she pat to my gravat,
The tither to my p—t—e, O.

Green grow, &c.

I dought na speak, yet was na fly'd.
My heart play'd duntie, duntie, 0,
A' ceremonie laid aside,
I fairly faund her c—t—ie, O.

Green grow, &c.

THE JOLLY GAUGER.
Tune—"*We'll gang nae mair a rovin*"
Anonymous. A close parody on "There was a jolly beggar," ascribed to King James V.

There was a jolly gauger, an' a gaugin' he did ride,
And he has met a beggar lass down by yon river side;
An' we'll gang nae mair a rovin' wi' ladies to the wine,
When a beggar wi' her meal-pocks can fidge her tail sae fine.

Amang the broom he laid her, amang the broom sae green,
And he's fa'n to the beggar, as she had been a queen;
An' we'll gang nae mair a rovin' wi' ladies to the wine,
When a beggar wi' her meal-pocks can fidge her tail sae fine.

My blessings on thee, laddie, thou's done my turn sae weel,
Wilt thou accept, dear laddie, my pock and pickle meal?
An' we'll gang nae mair a rovin' wi' ladies to the wine,
When a beggar wi' her meal-pocks can fidge her tail sae fine.

Sae blythe the beggar took the bent, like ony bird in spring,
Sae blythe the beggar took the bent, and merrily did sing;
An' we'll gang nae mair a rovin' wi' ladies to the wine,
When a beggar wi' her meal-pocks can fidge her tail sae fine.

My blessings on the gauger, o' gaugers he's the chief;
Sic kail ne'er crost my kettle, nor sic a joint o' beef;
An' we'll gang nae mair a rovin' wi' ladies to the wine,
When a beggar wi' her meal-pocks can fidge her tail sae fine.

NINE INCH WILL PLEASE A LADY.
Tune—"*The Quaker's Wife*,"
Anonymous, but evidently old; perhaps brushed up a little.

Come rede me, dame, come tell me, dame,
  My dame, come tell me truly.
What length o' graith, when weel ca'd hame,
  Will ser'e a woman duly?
The carlin clew her wanton tail,
  Her wanton tail sae ready;
I learn't a sang in Annandale,
  Nine inch will please a lady.

But for a countrie c—t like mine.
  In sooth we're nae sae gentle;
We'll tak' twa thumb-bread to the nine,
  And that's a sonsie p—t—e.
O leeze me on my Charlie lad!
  I'll ne'er forget my Charlie!
Twa roarin' handfu' and a daud,
  He nidg't it in fu' rarely.

But weary fa' the laithern doup.
  And may it ne'er ken thrivin';
It's no the length that gars me loup.
  But it's the double drivin'.
Come nidge me Tam, come nodge me Tam,
  Come nidge me o'er the nyvle;
Come louse and lug your batterin' ram.
  And thrash him at my gyvel.

HAD I THE WYTE SHE BADE ME.

An old song, of which there is more than one version. The setting of the "servant man and the lady" is common to many free songs of the kind, some of which are still current in Ayrshire. An amended version will be found in the Aldyne edition of 1893. The same version appears in Scott Douglas's 6 vol. edition (Vol. III., p. 270), with a note to the effect that it superseded the old song.   Had I the wyte, had I the wyte,
Had I the wyte she bade me;
 For she was steward in the house,
And I was fit-man laddie;
 And when I wadna do't again,
A silly cow she ca'd me;
 She straik't my head, and clapt my cheeks.
And lous'd my breeks and bade me.

 Could I for shame, could I for shame.
Could I for shame denied her;
 Or in the bed was I to blame
She bade me lye beside her:
 I pat six inches in her wame,
A quarter wadna fly'd her;
 For ay the mair I ca'd it hame.
Her ports they grew the wider.

 My tartan plaid when it was dark,
Could I refuse to share it;
 She hfted up her holland sark.
And bade me fin the gair o't:
 Or how could I amang the gerse.
But gie her hilt and hair o't;
 She clasped her houghs about my a—e.
And ay she glowr'd for mair o't.

ELLIBANKS.
Tune—"*Gillicrankie.*"

An old song, which appeared in the "Dublin Collection" (1769). Burns evidently meditated a purified version, for he writes to Robert Ainslie (November, 1791) a melancholy and penitential letter, in which this passage occurs—"I began 'Elibanks and Elibraes,' but the stanzas fell unenjoyed and unfinished from my listless tongue." On his Border tour, he saw "Elibanks and Elibraes on the other side of the Tweed," on which one of his editors (Scott Douglas) remarks— "An old free-spoken song which celebrates this locality would be enough in itself to bring the poet twenty miles out of his road to see it."   Elibanks and Elibraes,

My blessin's ay befa' them,
Tho' I wish I had brunt a' my claes,
The first time e'er I saw them;
Your succar kisses were sae sweet,
Deil haet if I can tell, man,
How ye gart me lay my legs abreed,
And lift my sark mysel', man.

There's no a lass in a' the land,
Can f—k sae weel as I can;
Louse down your breeks, lug out your wand,
Hae ye nae mind to try, man;
For ye're the lad that wears the breeks,
And I'm the lass that loes ye;
Deil rive my c—t to candle-wicks
Gif ever I refuse ye!!

I'll clasp my arms about your neck,
As I were gaun to speel, jo;
I'll cleek my houghs about your a—e,
As souple as an eel, jo;
I'll cleek my houghs about your a—e.
As I were gaun to speel, jo;
And if Jock thief he should slip out,
I'll ding him wi' my heel, jo.

        Green be the broom on Ellibraes,
And yellow be the gowan!
My wame it fistles ay like fleas.
As I come o'er the knowe, man;
My blessin's on that bonny knowe,
Our bed amang the heather.
Where sic a tuip to sic a ewe.
Was never matched thegither.

There I lay glowran to the moon.

Your mettle wadna daunton,
For hard your hurdies hotch'd aboon,
While I below lay pantin'.

The following is a M.S. version recovered by Scott Douglas:—

O Elibanks and Elibraes,
My blessin's aye befa' them,
They mind me o' the sunny days,
When first wi' thee I saw them,
Your succar kisses were sae sweet,
Deil haet if I can tell, man,
How ye gart me lay my legs abreed,
And lift my sark mysel', man.

I clasped my arms about your neck,
As I were gaun tae spiel, jo,
And cleek'd my houghs about your thies,
As souple as an eel, jo.
Your wauly p—t—e felt my grip
And made my senses reel, jo.
And when Jock thief inclin'd to slip,
I dang him wi' my heel, jo.

Oure Elibanks and Elibraes,
We wander'd at our will, jo.
Till tir'd o' pu'in' nits and slaes,
We drank of love our fill, jo;
My shepherd laddie, bless his breeks,
Kens whatna lassie loes him,
Deil rive my c—t to candle-weeks,
Gif ever I refuse him.

COMING O'ER THE HILLS O' COUPAR.

Tune—"*Ruffian's Rant.*"

An old song with internal evidence that it hails from the East coast.

Coming o'er the Hills o' Coupar,
Coming o'er the Hills o' Coupar,
Donald in a sudden wrath,
Ran his Highland dirk into her.

Donald Brodie met a lass,
Coming o'er the Hills o' Coupar,
Donald wi' his Highland wand.
Sounded a' the bits about her.

Coming o'er, &c.

Weel I wat she was a quean
Wad mak' a body's mouth to water;
Our mess John, wi's auld grey pow,
His holy lips wad lickit at her.

Coming o'er, &c.

Up she started in a fright,
And o'er the braes what she could bicker,
Let her gang, said Donald now.
For in her a—e my shot is sicker.

Coming o'er, &c.

BROSE AND BUTTER.

An old song. Burns transferred the first two lines of the 4th stanza to another composition.

Jenny sits up in the laft,
  Jockey would fain be at her,
But there cam' a wind out o' the west,
  Made a' the winnocks to clatter.

  O gi'e my love brose, brose,
  O gi'e my love brose and butter,
  For nane in Carrick but him
  Can please a lassie better.

The lavrock lo'es the grass,
  The paitrick lo'es the stibble;
And hey for the gardener lad,
  To gully away wi' his dibble.

O gi'e my love, &c.

My daddie sent me to the hill,
  To pu' my minnie some heather,
And drive it in your fill,
  Ye're welcome to the leather.

O gi'e my love, &c.

The mouse is a merry wee beast,
  The moudiewart wants the een;
And O for a touch of the thing,
  I had in my nieve yestreen.

O gi'e my love, &c.

We a' were fou yestreen,
  The night shall be its brither,
And hey for a merry pin,
  To nail twa wames thegither.

O gi'e my love, &c.□

An old song which Burns's purified version completely superseded. There is an echo of "Errock Brae" in the third line of the chorus. Comin' thro' the rye, my jo.
☐An' comin' thro' the rye.
 She fand a staun o' staunin' graith,
☐Comin' thro' the rye.

 O gin a body meet a body,
☐Comin' thro' the rye;
 Gin a body f—k a body,
☐Need a body cry.

                              Comin', &c.☐

        Gin a body meet a body,
☐Comin' thro' the glen;
 Gin a body f—k a body.
☐Need the warld ken.

                              Comin', &c.☐

        Gin a body meet a body,
☐Comin' thro' the grain;
 Gin a body f—k a body,
☐C——s a body's ain.

                              Comin', &c.☐

        Gin a body meet a body.
☐By a body's sel,
 Whatna body f——s a body.
☐Wad a body tell.

                              Comin' &c.☐

        Mony a body meets a body,
☐They dare na weel avow;

Mony a body f——s a body.
☐ Ye wad na think it true.

Comin'. &c.☐

THE BOWER OF BLISS.
Tune—"*Logan Water*."

In a letter from Burns to Wm. Stewart, Closeburn, dated Ellisland, Wednesday evening, he writes—"I go for Ayrshire to-morrow, so cannot have the pleasure of meeting you for some time, but anxious for your spiritual welfare and growth in grace, I enclose you the Plenipo. You will see another, the "Bower of Bliss," 'tis the work of a Rev. Doctor of the Church of Scotland. Would to Heaven a few more of them would turn their fiery zeal that way. There they might spend their holy fury, and show the tree by its fruits! ! ! There, the inbearing workings might give hopeful presages of a new birth! ! ! ! The other two are by the author of the Plenipo. 'The Doctor' is not half there, as I have mislaid it. I have no copies left of either, so must have the precious pieces again." This shows the part played by the poet's boon companions in the compilation of the Crochallan collection. The Plenipo did not find a place in the printed volume, but it was inserted in subsequent editions of the "Merry Muses." Its author was a Captain Morris, author of "Songs Drinking, Political and Facetious," published *circa* 1790.

The "high-kilted" muse does not become drawing-room costume. The deliberate, downright, mother-naked coarseness of the vernacular is infinitely preferable to this sickening stuff, which is Greek to the peasant, who calls a spade a spade because he has no other word for it.

Whilst others to thy bosom rise,
And paint the glories of thine eyes,
Or bid thy lips and cheeks disclose
The unfading bloom of Eden's rose;
Less obvious charms my song inspire
Which gods and men alike admire—
Less obvious charms, not less divine,
I sing that lovely bower of thine.

Rich gem! worth India's wealth alone,
How much pursued, how little known;
Tho' rough its face, tho' dim its hue,
It soils the lustre of Peru.
The vet'ran such a prize to gain.
Might all the toils of war sustain;
The devotee forsake his shrine,
To venerate that bower of thine.

When the stung heart feels keen desire,
And through each vein pours liquid fire;
When with flush'd cheeks and burning eyes,
Thy lover to thy bosom flies;
Believe, dear maid, believe my vow,
By Venus' self, I swear, 'tis true!
More bright the higher beauties shine,

Illum' d by that strange bower of thine.

What thought sublime, what lofty strain
Its wondrous virtues can explain?
No place howe'er remote, can be
From its intense attraction free;
Tho' more elastic far than steel.
Its force ten thousand needles feel;
Pleas'd their high temper to resign,
In that magnetic bower of thine.

Irriguous vale, embrown'd with shades,
Which no intrinsic storm pervades!
Soft clime, where native summer glows!
And nectar's living current flows!
Not Tempe's vale, renowned of yore,
Of charms could boast such endless store:
More than Elysian sweets combine,
To grace that smiling bower of thine.

O may no rash invader stain,
Love's warm, sequestered virgin fane!
For me alone let gentle fate,
Preserve the dear august retreat!
Along its banks when shall I stray?
The beauteous landscape when survey?
How long in fruitless anguish pine,
Nor view unveil'd that bower of thine.

O! let my tender, trembling hand,
The awful gate of life expand!
With all its wonders feast my sight;
Dear prelude to immense delight!
Till plung'd in liquid joy profound,
The dark unfathom'd deep I sound;
All panting on thy breast recline,
And, murmuring, bless that bower of thine.

AS I CAME O'ER THE CAIRNEY MOUNT.

An old song. A purified version by Burns will be found in Scott Douglas's Kilmarnock edition (Vol. II., p. 29). Burns writes to Thomson (Sept., 1793), "There is a third tune, and what Oswald calls 'The Old Highland Laddie,' which pleases me more than either of them; it is sometimes called 'Jinglin' Johnie,' that being the air of an old humorous bawdy song of that name—you will find it in the *Museum*." In the Genriddel MS. he says: "The 'Highland Laddie' is an excellent but somewhat licentious song beginning, 'As I cam' o'er the Cairney Mount.'" As I came o'er the Cairney mount,
And down amang the blooming heather,
 The Highland laddie drew his dirk
And sheath'd it in my wanton leather.

O my bonnie, bonnie Highland lad,
My handsome, charming Highland laddie;
 When I am sick and like to die,
He'll row me in his Highland plaidie.

 With me he play'd his warlike pranks,
And on me boldly did adventure,
 He did attack me on both flanks,
And pushed me fiercely in the centre.

O my bonnie, &c.

 A furious battle then began,
Wi' equal courage and desire,
 Altho' he struck me three to one,
I stood my ground and receiv'd his fire.

O my bonnie, &c.

 But our ammunition being spent,
And we quite out o' breath an' sweating,
 We did agree with ae consent,
To fight it out at the next meeting.

O my bonnie, &c.

SUPPER IS NOT READY.
Tune—"*Clout the Cauldron.*"
This is an old fragment.

Roseberry to his Lady says,
 My hinnie and my succar,
 O shall we do the thing you ken?
 Or shall we take our supper?

Fal lal, &c.

Wi' modest face, sae full of grace,
 Reply'd his bonny Lady,
 "My noble Lord, do as you please,
 But supper is not ready."

Fal lal, &c.

YON, YON, YON, LASSIE.
Tune—"*Ruffian's Rant*."
An old song.

O, yon, yon, yon, lassie,
Yon, yon, yon,
I never met a bonny lass,
But I wad play at yon.

O yon, yon, &c.

I never saw a silken gown,
But I wad kiss the sleeve o't;
I never saw a maidenhead,
That I wad spier the leave o't.

O yon, yon, &c.

Tell na me o' Meg my wife,
Her crowdie has na savour,
But gie to me a bonny lass,
And let me steal the favour.

O yon, yon, &c.

Gie me her I kissed yestreen,
I vow but she was handsome,
For ilka hair upon her c—t,
Was worth a royal ransom.

O yon, yon, &c.

THE YELLOW, YELLOW YORLIN'.
Tune—*"Bonnie beds of roses,"* or rather *"The Collier Laddie."*
An old song.

It fell on a day, in the flow'ry month o' May,
☐All on a merry, merry morning,
 I met a pretty maid, an' unto her I said,
☐I wad fain fin' your yellow, yellow yorlin'.

O no, young man, says she, you're a stranger to me,
☐An' I am my faither's darlin',
 I am herding his ewes that's feedin' in the howes,
☐An' ye maunna touch my yellow, yellow yorlin'.

But if I lay you down upon the dewy ground,
☐You wad na be the waur ae farthin';
 An' your faither, honest man, he never cou'd ken
☐That I play'd wi' your yellow, yellow yorlin'.

O fie, young man, says she, I pray you let me be,
☐I wad na for five pound sterling;
 My mither wad gae mad, an' sae wad my dad,
☐If you play'd wi' my yellow, yellow yorlin'.

But I took her by the waist, an' laid her down in haste,
☐For a' her squakin' an' squalin';
 The lassie soon grew tame, an' bade me come again
☐For to play wi' her yellow, yellow yorlin'.

THE SUMMER MORN.
Tune—"*Push about the Jorum.*"

This is by Burns. The following is what he wrote to Thomson regarding it in January, 1795:—
"To wander a little from my first design, which was to give you a new song just hot from the mint, give me leave to squeeze in a clever anecdote of my *Spring* originality. Some years ago, when I was young and by no means the saint I am now, I was looking over, in company with a *belle lettre* friend, a magazine 'Ode to Spring,' when my friend fell foul of the recurrence of the same thoughts, and offered me a bet that it was impossible to produce an ode to Spring on an original plan. I accepted it, and pledged myself to bring in the verdant fields, the budding flowers, the crystal streams, the melody of the groves, and a love story into the bargain, and yet be original. Here follows the piece, and wrote to music too." Along with this composition, he forwarded Thomson his immortal ode, "A man's a man for a' that." The second stanza is quoted in Scott Douglas's 5 vol. edition (Vol. III., p. 17), with but one word changed in the last line.

When maukin bucks, at early f—ks,
In dewy glens are seen, sir,
When birds on boughs tak aff their m—ws,
Amang the leaves sae green, sir,
Latona's son looks liquorish on
Dame Nature's grand impetus,
Till his p—t—e rise, then westward flies,
To f—k old Madame Thetis.

Yon wandering rill, that marks the hill,
And glances o'er the brae, sir,
Slides by a bower, where mony a flower
Sheds fragrance on the day, sir.
There Damon lay with Silvia gay,
To love they thought nae crime, sir,
The wild birds sang, the echoes rang,
While Damon's a—e beat time, sir.

First wi' the thrush, he thrust and pushed,.
His p—t—e large and strong, sir,
The blackbird next, his tunefu' text,
Made him both bold and strong, sir.
The linnet's lay came then in play,
And the lark that soared aboon, sir,
Till Damon fierce, mistimed his a—e,
And spent quite out of tune, sir.

SHE GRIPPET AT THE GIRTEST O'T.
Tune—"*East Neuk o' Fife.*"
An old song.

Our bride flat and our bride flang,
But lang before the laverock sang,
She paid him twice for every bang,
☐And grippet at the girtest o't.

Our bride turn'd her to the wa',
But lang before the cock did craw,
She took him by the cock and a'.
☐And grippet at the girtest o't.

WHA'LL MOW ME NOW?
Tune—"*Coming through the Rye.*"
An old song.

O wha'll mow me now, my jo.
　And wha'll mow me now,
　A sodger with his bandileers
　Has bang'd my belly fou.

　O I hae tint my rosy cheek,
　Likewise my waist sae sma',
　O wae gae wi' the sodger loon,
　The sodger did it a'.

                    And wha'll, &c.

　　For I maun thole the scornfu' sneer,
　O mony a saucy queen.
　When, curse upon her godly face,
　Her c——'s as merry's mine.

                    And wha'll, &c.

　　Our dame holds up her wanton tail,
　As oft as she down lies,
　And yet misca's a young thing,
　The trade if she but tries.

                    And wha'll, &c.

　　Our dame has aye her ain gudeman,
　And f——s for glutton greed,
　And yet misca's a poor thing,
　That f——s for its bread.

                    And wha'll, &c.

Alack! sae sweet a tree as love,

Sae bitter fruit should bear,
Alas! that e'er a merry c—t,
 Should draw so mony a tear.

                    And wha'll, &c.

        But devil tak' the lousy loon,
 Denies the bairn he got,
Or leaves the merry lass he lo'ed,
 To wear a ragged coat.

                    And wha'll, &c.

JOHN ANDERSON MY JO.

This is the old song which Burns's purified version superseded. The first two lines of the last stanza occur in "Annie Laurie."

John Anderson my jo, John,
☐I wonder what you mean,
To rise so soon in the morning,
☐And sit up so late at e'en?
You'll blear out all your een, John.
☐And why will you do so?
Come sooner to your bed at e'en,
☐John Anderson my jo.

John Anderson my friend, John,
☐When first you did begin,
You had as good a tail-tree
☐As ony ither man.
But now 'tis waxen auld, John,
☐And it waggles to and fro;
And it never stands its lane now,
☐John Anderson my jo.

John Anderson my jo, John,
☐You can f—k where'er you please,
Either in our warm bed,
☐Or else aboon the claise;
Or you shall have the horns, John,
☐Upon your head to grow;
That is a cuckold's malison,
☐John Anderson my jo.

So when you want to f—k, John,
☐See that you do your best,
When you begin to sh—g me,
☐See that you grip me fast;
See that you grip me fast, John,
☐Until that I cry Oh!
Your back shall crack, e'er I cry slack,
☐John Anderson my jo.

Oh! but it is a fine thing
☐To keek out o'er the dyke.
But 'tis a muckle finer thing,
☐When I see your hurdies fyke;
When I see your hurdies fyke, John,
☐And wriggle to and fro;
'Tis then I like your chaunter-pipe,

John Anderson my jo.

I'm backit like a salmon,
I'm breasted like a swan,
My wame it is a down cod,
My middle you may span;
From my crown until my tae, John,
I'm like the new-fa'n snow;
And 'tis a' for your conveniency,
John Anderson my jo.

A HOLE TO HIDE IT IN.
Tune—"*Waukin' o' the Fauld.*"
An old song.

O will ye speak at our town,
 As ye come frae the fair,
 And ye'se got a hole to hide it in,
 Will haud it a' and mair.

O haud awa' your hand, sir,
 Ye gar me aye think shame,
 And ye'se got a hole to hide it in,
 And think yoursel' at hame.

O will ye let me be, sir,
 Toots! now ye've reft my sark,
 And ye'se got a hole to hide it in,
 Whar ye may work your wark.

O haud awa' your hand, sir,
 Ye're like to make me daft,
 And ye'se got a hole to hide it in
 To keep it warm and saft.

O haud it in your hand, sir,
 Till I get up my claes,
 Now f—k me as you'd f—k for life,
 I hope your cock will please.

DUNCAN MACLEERIE.
Tune—"*Jockey Macgill.*"
An old song.

Duncan Macleerie and Janet his wife,
They gaed to Kilmarnock to buy a new knife,
But instead of a knife they coft but a bleerie,
We're very well saired, Janet, quoth Duncan Macleerie.

Duncan Macleerie has got a new fiddle,
It's a' strung wi' hair, and a hole in the middle,
And aye when he plays on't his wife looks sae cheerie,
Weel done, my Duncan, quoth Janet Macleerie.

Duncan he played till his bow it grew greasy,
Janet grew fretfu' and unco uneasy,
Hoots! quoth she, Duncan, ye're unco soon weary,
Play us a pibroch, quoth Janet Macleerie.

Duncan Macleerie he played on the harp,
Janet Macleerie she danced in her sark,
Her sark it was short, her c—t it was hairy,
Very weel danced, Janet, quoth Duncan Macleerie.

DUNCAN DAVIDSON
An old song. Burns's purified version is well known.

There was a lass, they ca'd her Meg,
☐And she gaed o'er the muir to spin,
She fee'd a lad to lift her leg,
☐They ca'ed him Duncan Davidson.

Fal lal, &c.

Meg had a muff, and it was rough,
☐'Twas black without and red within,
And Duncan, 'cause he'd got a cauld,
☐He slipt his Highland p—t—e in.

Fal lal, &c.

Meg had a muff, and it was rough,
☐And Duncan stuck twa nievefu' in.
Meg clapped her heels about his waist,
☐"I thank ye, Duncan, yerk it in."

Fal lal, &c.

Duncan made her hurdies dreep,
☐Brise 'yont, my lad, then Meg did say:
O gang he east, or gang he west.
☐My c—t will not be dry the day.

Fal lal, &c.

O SAW YE MY MAGGY?
Tune—*"Saw ye my Maggy."*
An old song.

O saw ye my Maggy,
O saw ye my Maggy,
O saw ye my Maggy,
Coming o'er the lea?

What mark has your Maggy,
What mark has your Maggy,
What mark has your Maggy,
That ane may ken her by?

My Maggy has a mark,
You'll find it in the dark,
It's in below her sark,
A little aboon her knee.

What wealth has your Maggy
What wealth has your Maggy,
What wealth has your Maggy,
In tocher, gowd, or fee?

My Maggy has a treasure,
A hidden mine o' pleasure,
I'll dig it at my leisure,
It's a' alane for me.

How meet ye your Maggy,
How meet ye your Maggy,
How meet ye your Maggy,
When nane's to hear or see?

E'en that tell our wishes,
Eager glowing kisses,
Then, diviner blisses,
In holy ecstacy.

How lo'e ye your Maggy,
How lo'e ye your Maggy,
How lo'e ye your Maggy,
And lo'e nane but she?

Heavenly joys before me,
Rapture trembling o'er me,

Maggy, I adore thee,
□On my bended knee.

THEY TOOK ME TO THE HOLY BAND.
Tune—*"Clout the Cauldron."*
An old fragment.

They took me to the Holy Band,
For playing wi' my wife, sir,
And lang and sair they lectured me,
For leading sic a life, sir.

I answered in not many words,
"What deil needs a' this clatter?
As long as she could keep the grig,
I aye was f——g at her."

THE PLOUGHMAN.

An old song. A purified version will be found in Herd (Vol. II., p. 144). William Scott Douglas prints another version in his Kilmarnock edition (Vol. I., p. 222). The parable of the "three owsen," begun in the fourth stanza, is found in the "Auld White Nag," a licentious ditty current in Ayrshire to this day, the "owsen" being changed into "pownies." It also is evidently old.

> "Then he drew out his horses which were in number three,
> Three likelier pownies for to draw, their like ye ne'er did see.
> There was twa dun pownies on ahin', auld Whitey on afore,
> The muzzle-pin for a' the yirth was in the highest bore."

> "Before he gat the hause-rig turned his horse began to sweat,
> And to maintain an open fur, he spurred wi' baith his feet," &c.

The ploughman he's a bonny lad,
His mind is ever true, jo,
His garters knit below his knee.
His bonnet it is blue, jo.

Then up wi't a', my ploughman lad,
And hey my merry ploughman.
Of a' the trades that I do ken,
Commend me to the ploughman.

As walking forth upon a day,
I met a jolly ploughman.
I told him I had lands to plough,
If he wad prove a true man.

He says, my dear, take ye nae fear,
I'll fit ye to a hair, jo,
I'll cleave it up, and hit it down,
And water-furrow' t fair, jo.

I hae three owsen in my plough.
Three better ne'er plough'd ground, 3jo;
The foremost ox is lang and sma',
And twa are plump and round, jo.

Then he wi' speed did yoke his plough,
Which by a gaud was driven, jo.
And when he was between the stilts,
He thought he was in heaven, jo.

But the foremost ox fell in the fur,
The tither twa did flounder, jo,
The ploughman lad he breathless grew,

In troth it was nae wonder, jo.

But sic a risk below a hill,
The plough she took a stane, jo.
Which gart the fire flee frae the stock.
The ploughman gaed a grane, jo.

I hae plough'd east, I hae plough'd west.
In weather foul and fair, jo,
But the sairest ploughing e'er I plough'd,
Was ploughing amang hair, jo.

Sing up wi't a', and in wi't a',
And hey my merry ploughman,
O' a' the trades and crafts I ken,
Commend me to the ploughman.

HOW CAN I KEEP MY MAIDENHEAD.
Tune—"*The Birks o' Abergeldie*."
An old song.

    How can I keep my maidenhead,
My maidenhead, my maidenhead;
How can I keep my maidenhead,
  Among sae mony men, O.

The captain bad a guinea for't,
A guinea for't, a guinea for't;
The captain bad a guinea for't,
  The colonel he bad ten, O.

But I'll do as my minnie did,
My minnie did, my minnie did;
But I'll do as my minnie did,
  For siller I'll hae nane, O.

I'll gie it to a bonie lad,
A bonie lad, a bonie lad;
I'll gie it to a bonie lad,
  For just as gude again, O.

An auld moulie maidenhead,
A maidenhead, a maidenhead;
An auld moulie maidenhead,
  The weary wark I ken, O.

The stretchin' o't, the strivin' o't,
The borin' o't, the rivin' o't,
And ay the double drivin' o't,
  The farther ye gang ben, O.

DAINTY DAVY.

This appears in Herd's collection (1776). It refers to an incident of the Covenanting times. Mr. David Williamson, a minister of the Covenant, being pursued by the dragoons, took refuge in Lady Cherrytree's house, who, the better to conceal him, put him to bed beside her daughter, whom he got with child, to the great scandal of the Puritans of that period. In a letter to Thomson, Burns refers to its "wit and humour entitling it to a place in any collection."

O leeze me on his curly pow,
Bonie Davie, dainty Davie;
Leeze me on his curly pow,
He was my dainty Davie.

Being pursued by the dragoons,
Within my bed he was laid down,
And weel I wat he was worth his room,
My ain dear dainty Davie.

Leeze me, &c.

My minnie laid him at my back,
I trow he lay na lang at that,
But turn'd, and in a verra crack
Produc'd a dainty Davie.

Leeze me, &c.

Then in the field among the pease,
Behin' the house o' Cherrytrees,
Again he wan atweesh my thies,
And creesh'd them weel wi' gravy.

Leeze me, &c.

But had I goud, or had I land,
I should be a' at his command;
I'll ne'er forget what he pat i' my hand,
It was sic a dainty Davie.

Leeze me, &c.

THE MOUDIWARK.

Tune—*"O for ane and twenty Tam."*
An old song.

  The moudiwark has done me ill,
And below my apron has biggit a hill,
I maun consult some learned clark,
About this wanton moudiwark.

☐And O the wanton moudiwark,
☐The weary wanton moudiwark,
☐I maun consult my learned clark,
☐About this wanton moudiwark.

O first it gat between my taes,
 Out o'er my garter neist it gaes,
 At length it crap below my sark,
The weary wanton moudiwark.

      And O the, &c.☐

This moudiwark, tho' it be blin',
If ance the nose o't you let in,
Then to the hilts, within a crack,
The weary wanton moudiwark,

      And O the, &c.☐

When Marjorie was made a bride,
And Willie lay down by her side.
Syne nought was heard when it was dark,
But kicking at the moudiwark.

      And O the, &c.☐

ANDREW AND HIS CUTTY GUN.

An old song which Burns describes as "the work of a master." Burns's purified version is well known. An amended version will be found in Herd's collection (1776).   Blythe, blythe, blythe was she,
　Blythe was she but and ben,
 And weel she loved it in her neeve,
　But better when it slippit in.

Blythe. blythe, &c.

　　When a' the lave gaed to their bed,
　And I sat up to clean the shoon,
 O wha think ye came jumpin' ben,
　But Andrew and his cutty gun.

Blythe. blythe, &c.

　　Or e'er I wist he laid me back,
　And up my gamon to my chin,
 And ne'er a word to me he spak,
　But liltit out his cutty gun.

Blythe. blythe, &c.

　　The bawsent bitch she left her whelps,
　And hunted round us at the fun,
 As Andrew dougled wi' his doup,
　And fired at me his cutty gun.

Blythe. blythe, &c.

　　O some delight in cutty-stoup,
　And some delight in cutty-mum,
 But my delight's an arselins coup,
　Wi' Andrew and his cutty gun.

Blythe. blythe, &c.

THE MILL, MILL, O.

"The original," says Burns in the Glenriddel MS., "or at least a song evidently prior to
Ramsay's, is still extant. It runs thus, "'As I came down yon water side,' &c."
From this Burns evolved the "Soldier's Return."

As I came down yon water side,
  And by yon shillin hill, O;
There I spied a bonny lass,
  A lass that I lo'ed right weel, O.

  The mill, mill, O, and the kill, kill, O,
  An' the coggin' o' Peggy's wheel, O,
  The sack and the seive, an' a' she did leave,
  An' danced the miller's reel, O.

I spier'd at her, gin she could play,
  But the lassie had nae skill, O;
An' yet she was nae a' to blame,
  She pat it in my will, O.

                    The mill, mill, O, &c.

Then she fell o'er, an' sae did I,
  An' danced the miller's reel, O,
Whene'er that bonny lassie comes again,
  She shall hae her maut ground weel, O.

                    The mill. mill. O. &c.

O GAT YE ME WI' NAETHING.
An old song.

"Gat ye me, O gat ye me,
　And gat ye me wi' naething.
A rock, a reel, a spinning wheel,
　A gude black c—t was ae thing.

"A tocher fine, o'er muckle far,
　When sic a scallion gat it."
"Indeed o'er muckle far, gudewife,
　For that was aye the faut o't.

"But haud your tongue now, Luckie Laing,
　O haud your tongue and jander.
I held the gate till you I met,
　Syne I began to wander.

"I tint my whistle and my sang,
　I tint my peace and pleasure,
But your green grave now, Luckie Laing,
　Wad airt me to my treasure."

CAN YE LABOUR LEA, YOUNG MAN?
Tune—*"Sir Arch. Grant's Strathspey."*

An old song, of which there are many versions. The title appears to have been a favourite with the old rhymers.

O can ye labour lea, young man?
　O can ye labour lea?
Gae back the road ye came again,
　Ye ne'er shall scorn me.

I fee'd a man at Martinmas,
　Wi' arle pennies three,
But a' the faut I had to him,
　He couldna labour lea.

O can ye, &c.

A stibble rig is easy ploughed,
　And fallow land is free,
But what a silly coof is he,
　That couldna labour lea.

O can ye, &c.

The bonny bush and benty knowe,
　The ploughman points his sock in,
He sheds the roughness, lays it by.
　And bauldly ploughs his yoking.

O can ye, &c.

OUR JOCK'S BRACK YESTREEN.
Tune—*"Gramachree."*
An old song.

Twa neighbour wives sat in the sun,
  A twining at their rocks,
And they an argument began,
  And a' the plea was cocks.

'Twas whether they were sinews strong,
  Or whether they were bane,
And how they rowed about your thumb,
  And how they stood their lane.

First Rachel gied her rock a tug,
  And syne she claw'd her tail,
 "When our Tam draws on his breeks,
  It waggles like a flail."

Says Bess, "They're bane, I will maintain,
  And proof in point I'll gie,
 For our Jock's cock it brak yestreen,
  And I found it on my thigh."

SHE ROSE AND LOOT ME IN.

The old version is by Semple of Beltrees, and appears in Ramsay's "Tea-Table Miscellany," the "Orpheus Caledonius," and "Herd's Collection." In the Glenriddel MS. Burns says, "The old set of this song, which is still to be found in printed collections, is much prettier than this; but somebody (I believe it was Ramsay) took it into his head to clear it of some seeming indelicacies, and made it at once more chaste and more dull." On 7th April, 1793, he writes to Thomson—"I shall be extremely sorry if you set any other song to the air 'She rose and loot me in,' except the song of that title. It would be cruel to spoil the allusion in poor, unfortunate M'Donald's pretty ode." The amended version first appeared in a collection called "The Blackbird," in 1764.

The night her silent sable wore,
An' gloomin' was the skies;
O' glittrin' stars appeared no more
Than those in Nelly's eyes:
When at her father's gate I knocked,
Where I had often been;
Shrouded only in her smock,
She rose and loot me in.

Fast lock'd within my fond embrace,
She tremblin' stood asham'd;
Her glowin' lips an' heaving breasts,
At every touch enflam'd;
My eager passion I obeyed,
Resolved the fort to win;
An' she, at last, gave her consent
To yield an' let me in.

O then! what bliss beyond compare,
I knew no greater joy;
Enroll'd in heavenly happiness,
So bless't a man was I;
An' she, all ravished with delight,
Bad me aft come again,
An' kindly vow'd, that ev'ry night
She'd rise and let me in.

But ah! at last she prov'd wi' bairn,
An' sat baith sad and dull,
An' I wha was as much concerned
Looked e'en just like a fool;
Her lovely eyes wi' tears ran o'er,
Repentin' her rash sin;
An' ay she cursed the fatal hour

That e'er she loot me in.

But who could from such beauty go,
Or yet from Nelly part;
I lov'd her dear, an' cou'dna leave
The charmer of my heart,
We wedded and conceal'd our crime,
Then all was weel again,
An' she doth bless the happy night
She rose an' loot me in

GIE THE LASS HER FAIRING.
Tune—*"Cauld Kail in Aberdeen."*
An old fragment.

O gie the lass her fairing, lad,
　O gie the lass her fairing;
And something else she'll gie to you,
　That's wallow worth the wearing.
Syne coup her o'er amang the creels,
　When ye hae ta'en your brandy,
The mair you bang, the less she squeals,
　So hey for houghmagandie.

Then gie the lass her fairing, lad,
　O gie the lass her fairing,
And she'll gie you a hairy thing,
　And of it be not sparing,
Lay her o'er amang the creels,
　And bar the door wi' baith your heels,
The mair she gets, the less she squeals,
　So hey for houghmagandie.

POOR BODIES DO NAETHING BUT MOW.
Tune—*"The Campbells are Coming."*

This is by Burns. Writing to Cleghorn (December 12, 1792), he says—"By our good friend Crossbie, I send you a song just finished this moment. May the d——l follow with a blessing. Amen!" To Thomson, in July, 1794, he writes—"The needy man, who has known better times, can only console himself with a song, thus—   'While princes and prelates,' &c,"
When he was called in question about his political opinions, he wrote the following to Graham of Fintry (January 5, 1793)—"A tippling ballad which I made on Prince of Brunswick's breaking up his camp, and sung one convivial evening, I shall likewise send you, sealed up, as it's not for everybody's reading. This last is not worth your perusal; but lest Mrs. Fame should, as she has already done, use and even abuse her old privilege of lying, you shall be the master of everything, *le pour et le contre*, of my political writings and conduct."

When princes and prelates,
And hot-headed zealots
A' Europe had set in a lowe, lowe, lowe,
The poor man lies down,
Nor envies a crown,
But contents himself wi' a mow, mow, mow.

And why shouldna poor bodies mow, mow, mow?
And why shouldna poor bodies mow?
The rich they hae siller, and houses, and land,
Poor bodies hae naething but mow.

When Brunswick's great Prince
Gaed a crushing to France,
Republican billies to cow, cow, cow,
Great Brunswick's strange Prince
Would have shown better sense,
At hame wi' his Princess to mow, mow, mow.

And why shouldna, &c.

The Emperor swore,
By sea and by shore,
At Paris to kick up a row, row, row,
But Paris aye ready,
Just laughed at the laddie,
And bid him gae hame, and gae mow, mow, mow.

And why shouldna, &c.

When the brave Duke of York

The Rhine first did pass,
Republican armies to cow, cow, cow,
They bid him gae hame
To his Prussian dame,
And gie her a kiss and a mow, mow, mow.

And why shouldna, &c.

Out over the Rhine
Proud Prussia did shine,
To spend his last blade he did vow, vow, vow,
But Frederick had better
Ne'er forded the water,
But spent as he ought at a mow, mow, mow.

And why shouldna, &c.

The black-headed eagle,
As keen as a beagle,
He hunted o'er height, and o'er howe, howe, howe.
In the braes of Gemappe,
He fell into a trap,
E'en let him get out as he dow, dow, dow.

And why shouldna, &c.

When Kate laid her claws
On poor Stanislaus,
And his p—t—e was bent like a bow, bow, bow,
May the deil in her a——e
Ram a huge p——k of brass,
And send her to hell wi' a mow, mow, mow.

And why shouldna, &c.

Then fill up your glasses,
Ye sons of Parnassus,
This toast I'm sure you'll allow, allow,
Here's to Geordie our King,
And Charlotte his Queen,
And lang may they live for to mow, mow, mow.

And why shouldna, &c.

An alternative version of the last stanza.

But truce with commotions, and new fangled notions,
□*A bumper I trust you'll allow, allow;*
Here's George our good King, and long may he ring,
□*And Charlotte and he tak' a mow, mow, mow.*

□And why shouldna, &c.

THE COOPER O' CUDDY.
Tune—*"Bob at the Bowster."*

A MS. of this old song is in the British Museum, in the holograph of Burns; but it is not identical with the version here given. Probably he took it down as a later or preferable version.

The Cooper o' Cuddy cam' here awa',
He ca'd the girrs out o'er us a',
An' our gudewife has gotten a fa'
☐That angered the silly gudeman, O.

☐We'll hide the cooper behind the door,
☐Behind the door, behind the door,
☐We'll hide the cooper behind the door,
☐And cover him with a mawn. O.

He sought them out, he sought them in,
Wi' deil hae her, and deil hae him,
But the body he was sae doited an' blin',
☐He wistna where he was gaun, O.

☐We'll hide the cooper, &c.

They cooper'd at e'en—they cooper'd at morn,
Till our gudeman has gotten the scorn,
On ilka brow he's planted a horn,
☐And swears that there they shall stand, O.

☐We'll hide the cooper, &c.

THERE CAM' A CADGER.
Tune—*"Clout the Cauldron."*
An old fragment.

There cam' a cadger out o' Fife,
  I wat na how they ca'd him;
He play'd a trick to our gudewife,
  When fient a body bad him.

  Fal lal. &c.

He took a lang thing stout and strang,
  An' strack it at her gyvel;
An' aye she swore she fand the thing
  Gae borin' by her nyvel.

  Fal lal, &c.

KEN YE NA OUR LASS BESS.
Tune—*"Auld Sir Symon."*
An old song.

O, ken ye na our lass, Bess?
　An' ken ye na our lass, Bess?
Between her lily white thies
　She's biggit a magpie's nest.

An' ken ye na our lad, Tam?
　An' ken ye na our lad, Tam?
He's on a three-fitted stool,
　An' up to the nest he clamb.

An' what did he there, think ye?
　An' what did he there, think ye?
He brak a' the eggs o' the nest,
　An' the white's ran down her thie.

WHA THE DEIL CAN HINDER THE WIND TAE BLAW?
Tune—*"Wat ye wha I met yestreen."*

An old song. It looks as if it were filched from "The Grey Goose and the Gled," the last stanza especially.

It fell about the blythe New Year,
　When days are short and nights are lang,
Ae bonie night, the starns were clear,
　An' frost beneath my fit-stead rang;
I heard a carlin cry "relief!"
　Atweesh her trams a birkie lay;
But he wan a quarter in her beef,
　For a' the jirts the carlin gae.

She heaved tae, and he strak frae,
　As he wad nail'd the carlin thro';
An ilka f—t the carlin gae,
　It wad hae fill'd a pockie fou;
Temper your tail, the young man cried,
　Temper your tail by Venus' law I
Double your dunts, the dame replied,
　Wha the deil can hinder the wind tae blaw?

WE'RE A' GAUN SOUTHIE O.
Tune—*"The Merry lads of Ayr."*
An old song.

Callum cam to Campbell's court,
□An' saw ye e'er the make o't;
Pay'd twenty shillings for a thing,
□An' never got a straik o't.

□We're a' gaun southie O.
□We're a' gaun there;
□An' we're a' gaun to Mauchline fair,
□To sell our pickle hair.

Pay'd twenty shillings for a quine,
□Her name was Kirsty Lauchlan;
But Callum took her by the c—t,
□Before the laird o' Mauchline.

□We're a', &c.

Callum cam to Kirsty's door,
□Says, Kirsty are ye sleepin'?
No sae soun' as ye wad trow,
□Ye'se get the thing ye're seekin'.

□We're a', &c.

Callum had a peck o' meal,
□Says Kirsty, will ye draik it?
She whippit aff her wee white coat,
□An' birket at it nakit.

□We're a', &c.

Bonie lassie, braw lassie,
□Will ye hae a soger?
Then she took up her duddie sark,
□An' he shot in his Roger.

□We're a', &c.

Kind kimmer Kirsty,
□I lo'e wi' a' my heart, O,
An' when there's ony p—t—s gaun,

She'll ay get a part, O.

We're a', &c.

JOCKEY WAS A BONNY LAD.

Tune—*"John Roy Stewart's Strathspey."*

An old song which appears in the Appendix to Herd's collection.

My Jockey is a bonny lad,
A dainty lad, a merry lad,
A neat, sweet, pretty little lad,
　An' just the lad for me.
For when we o'er the meadows stray,
He's ay sae lively, ay sae gae,
An' aft right canty does he say,
　There's nane he lo'es like me.

　An' he's ay huggin', ay dawtin',
　Ay clappin', ay pressin',
　Ay squeezin', ay kissin',
　An' winna let me be.

I met my lad the ither day,
Friskin' thro' a field o' hay;
Says he, dear Jenny, will ye stay,
　An' crack a while wi' me.
No, Jockey lad, I darena stay,
My mither she'd miss me away;
Syne she'll flyte an' scauld a' day,
　An' play the deil wi' me.

　But Jockey still continued
　Ay huggin', &c.

Hoot! Jockey, see my hair is down,
An' look ye've torn a' my gown,
An' how will I gae thro' the town,
　Dear laddie tell to me.
He never minded what I said,
But wi' my neck an' bosom play'd;
Tho' I entreated, begg'd, an' pray'd
　Him no to touzle me.

　But Jockey still continued
　Huggin', dawtin', clappin', squeezin',
　An' aye kissin', kissin', kissin'.
　Till down cam we.
As breathless an' fatigued I lay,
In his arms among the hay,
My blood fast thro' my veins did play

As he lay huggin' me;
I thought my breath would never last,
For Jockey danc'd sae devilish fast;
But what cam o'er, I trow, at last,
There's deil ane kens but me.

But soon he wearied o' his dance,
O' a' his jumpin' an' his prance,
An' confess'd without romance,
He was fain to let me be.

MY AIN KIND DEARY.
An old song on which Burns modelled his beautiful lyric with the same title.

I'll lay thee o'er the lee-rig,
　Lovely Mary, dearie, O;
I'll lay thee o'er the lee-rig,
　My lovely Mary, dearie, O.
　Altho' the night were ne'er so wet,
　An' I were ne'er so weary O;
I'd lay thee o'er the lee-rig
　My lovely Mary, dearie, O.

　Altho' the night, &c.

　Look down ye gods from yonder sky,
　An' see how blest a man am I;
No envy my fond heart alarms,
　Encircled in my Mary's arms.
　Lyin' across the lee-rig,
　Wi' lovely Mary, dearie, O;
　Lyin' across the lee-rig
　Wi' my ain kind deary, O.

　Altho' the night, &c.

HERE'S HIS HEALTH IN WATER.
Tune—*"The job o' journey wark."*

An early production of Burns, on an old model, written, it is supposed, when Jean Armour was "under a cloud." The first verse appears in most editions of Burns's works.

Altho' my back be at the wa',
An' tho' he be the fautor;
Altho' my back be at the wa',
I'll drink his health in water.
O wae gae by his wanton sides,
Sae brawly's he could flatter.
Though for his sake I'm slighted sair,
An' dree the kintra clatter;
But let them say whate'er they like,
Yet, here's his health in water.

He followed me baith out and in,
Thro' a' the nooks o' Killie;
He followed me baith out and in,
Wi' a stiff stanin' pillie.
But when he gat atween my legs,
We made an unco splutter;
An' haith, I trow, I soupled it,
Tho' bauldly he did blatter;
But now my back is at the wa',
Yet here's his health in water.

ACT SEDERUNT OF THE COURT OF SESSION.
Tune—*"O'er the Muir amang the Heather."*

Burns wrote to Robert Cleghorn, under date October 25, 1793:—"I have just bought a quire of post, and I am determined, my dear Cleghorn, to give you the maidenhead of it. Indeed, that is all my reason for, and all that I can propose to give you by, the present scrawl. From my late hours last night, and the dripping fogs and damn'd east wind of this stupid day, I have left me as little soul as an oyster.—'Sir John, you are so fretful, you cannot live long.'—'Why, there is it! Come, sing me a b——dy song to make me merry!!'

"Act Sederunt o' the Session.   "Tune—*'O'er the muir amang the heather.'*

"Well, the Law is good for something, since we can make a b——dy song out of it. (N.B.—I never made anything of it any other way.) There is, there must be some truth in original sin. My violent propensity to b—dry convinces me of it. Lack a day! if that species of composition be the special sin, never-to-be-forgiven in this world nor in that which is to come, I am the most offending soul alive."   In Embro' town they've made a law,

☐In Embro' at the Court o' Session,
 That standin' p——s are fautor's a',
☐And guilty o' a high transgression.

☐Decreet o' the Court o' Session,
☐Act Sederunt o' the Session,
☐That standin' p——s are fautor's a',
☐And guilty o' a high transgression.

 And they've provided dungeons deep,
☐Ilk lass has ane in her possession,
 Until the fautors wail and weep,
☐There they shall lie for their transgression.

☐Decreet o' the Court o' Session,
☐Act Sederunt o' the Session.
☐The rogues in pouring tears shall weep,
☐By Act Sederunt o' the Session.

BLYTH WILL AND BESSIE'S WEDDING.
Tune—"*Roy's Wife.*"

An old song. The stanzas in brackets seem to be an interpolation from another ditty much resembling "Comin' o'er the hills o' Couper."

There was a wedding o'er in Fife,
 An' mony a ane frae Lothian at it;
Jean Vernon there maist lost her life,
 For love o' Jamie Howden at it.

Blyth Will and Bessie's weddin',
 Blyth Will and Bessie's weddin',
Had I been Will, Bess had been mine,
 An' Bess an' I had made the weddin'.

Right sair she grat, and wet her cheeks,
 An' naithing pleased that we could gie her;
She tint her heart in Jamie's breeks,
 It cam nae back to Lothian wi' her.

Blyth, &c.

[Kate Mackie cam frae Parloncraigs,
 The road was foul 'twixt that an' Couper;
She shaw'd a pair o' handsome legs.
 When Highland Donald he o'ertook her.

Comin' o'er the moor o' Couper,
 Coming o'er the moor o' Couper,
Donald fell in love wi' her.
 An' row'd his Highland plaid about her.

They took them to the Logan steps,
 An' set them down to rest thegither,
Donald laid her on her back.
 An' fir'd a Highland pistol at her.

Comin'. &c.

Lochleven Castle heard the rair,
 An' Faulkland house the echo sounded;
Highland Donald gae a stare.
 The lassie sigh'd, but was nae wounded.]

Comin', &c.

Tamie Tamson too was there,
Maggie Birnie was his dearie.
He pat it in amang the hair,
An' puddled there till he was weary.

Blyth, &c.

When e'enin' cam the town was thrang,
An' beds were no to get for siller;
When e'er they fand a want o' room,
They lay in pairs like bread and butter.

Blyth, &c.

Twa and twa they made the bed,
An' twa an' twa they lay thegither;
When they had na room enough,
Ilk ane lap on aboon the tither.

Blyth, &c.

AS I LOOKED O'ER YON CASTLE WA'.
Tune—"*Cumnock Psalms.*"

An old song. In a letter to Thomson, dated September, 1794, Burns says:—"Do you know a droll Scots song, more famous for its humour than delicacy, called 'The Grey Goose and the Gled.' Mr. Clark took down the notes (such as they are) at my request, which I shall give with some decenter verses to Johnson. Mr. Clark says that the tune is positively an old chant of the Romish Church, which corroborates the old tradition that at the Reformation the Reformers burlesqued much of the old church music with setting them to bawdy verses. As a further proof, the common name for this song is 'Cumnock Psalms.' As there can be no harm in transcribing a stanza of a psalm, I shall give you two or three; possibly the song is new to you:—
"Cumnock Psalms.

"'As I looked o'er yon castle wa',
I spied a grey goose and a gled,' &c.
So much for the psalmody of Cumnock."

As I looked o'er yon castle wa',
☐I spied a grey goose and a gled;
They had a feight between them twa,
☐An' O, as their twa hurdies gaed.

☐Wi' a hey ding it in, an' a how ding it in,
☐An' a hey ding it in, it's lang to-day.
☐Fal lary tele, tale, lary tale,
☐Fal lary tal, lal, lary tay.

She heav'd up and he strack down,
☐Between them twa they made a m—w;
And ilka fart that the carlin gae.
☐It's four o' them wad filled a bowe.

With a hey, &c.

Temper your tail the carle cried,
☐Temper your tale by Venus' law;
Gird hame your gear, gudeman, she cried,
☐Wha the deil can hinder the wind tae blaw.

With a hey, &c.

For were ye on my saddle set,

An' were ye weel girt in my gear,
 Gin the wind o' my a—e blaw ye out o' my c—t,
　Ye'll never be reckoned a man o' weir.

                                        With a hey, &c.

              He placed his Jacob whare she did piss,
An' his b—ks whare the wind did blaw.
And he grippet her fast by the gushet o' her a—e,
An' he gae her c—t the common law.

                                        With a hey, &c.

LOGAN WATER.

"An old song which appears in Herd's Collection. Referring to it, Burns writes to Thomson (April 7, 1793)—"I remember two ending lines of a verse in some of the old songs of 'Logan Water' (for I know a good many different ones) which I think pretty—

"'Now my dear lad maun face his faes,
☐Far, far frae me and Logan Braes.'"

The Logan burn, the Logan braes,
I helped a bonie lassie on wi' her claes;
First wi' her stockings an' syne wi' her shoon,
But she gied me the glaiks when a' was done.

But an I had ken'd what I ken now,
I wad a' bang'd her belly fu';
Her belly fu' and her apron up,
An' shew'd her the road to the Logan Kirk,

THE COOPER O' DUNDEE.
Tune—*"Bonnie Dundee."*
An old song.

Ye Coopers and Hoopers attend to my ditty,
I'll sing of a cooper who dwelt in Dundee,
This young man he was baith am'rous and witty,
He pleased the fair maids wi' the blink of his e'e.

He wasna a cooper, a common tub hooper,
The maist of his trade lay in pleasing the fair,
He hoop'd them, he coop'd them, he bor'd them, he plugg'd them,
And a' sent for Sandy when oot o' repair.

For a twelvemonth or so this youth was respected,
And he was as busy as weel he could be,
But business increas'd sae, that some were neglected,
Which ruined his trade in the town o' Dundee.

A bailie's fair daughter had wanted a coopin',
And Sandy was sent for, as ofttimes was he,
He yerk't her sae hard, that she sprung an end hoopin',
Which banish'd poor Sandy from bonny Dundee.

WHISTLE O'ER THE LAVE O'T.

A fragment of the old song on which Burns modelled his amended version.

My mither sent me to the well,
She had better gane hersel,
I got the thing I daur nae tell,
☐ Whistle o'er the lave o't.

My mither sent me to the sea,
For to gather mussles three;
A sailor lad fell in wi' me,
☐ Whistle o'er the lave o't.

THE RANTING DOG THE DADDY O'T.
Tune—*"East Neuk o' Fife."*

Concerning this composition, Burns himself says:—"I composed this song pretty early in life, and sent it to a young girl, a very particular acquaintance of mine, who was at that time under a cloud." This was doubtless Betty Paton, mother of his "dear bought Bess," at whose birth he composed "The Poet's Welcome." Both pieces are printed in most editions of Burns's works.

O wha my baby clouts will buy?
O wha will tent me when I cry?
O wha will kiss me where I lie?
　But the ranting dog the daddy o't.
O wha will own he did the faut?
O wha will buy the groaning maut?
O wha will tell me what to ca't?
　But the ranting dog the daddy o't.

When I mount the creepie chair,
Wha will sit beside me there?
Gie me Rab, I'll ask nae mair,
　The ranting dog the daddy o't.
Wha will crack to me my lane?
Wha will make me fidging fain?
Wha will kiss me o'er again?
　But the ranting dog the daddy o't.

JENNY MACRAW.
Tune—*"The bonny moorhen."*
An old song.

Jenny Macraw was a bird o' the game,
An' mony a shot had been lows'd at her wame;
Be't a lang bearing arrow, or the sharp-rattlin' hail,
Still, whirr! she flew off wi' the shot in her tail.

Jenny Macraw to the mountains she's gane,
Their leagues and their covenants a' she has ta'en;
"My head now, and heart now," quo she, "are at rest,
An' for my poor c—t, let the deil do his best."

Jenny Macraw on a midsummer morn,
She cut off her c—t and she hung't on a thorn;
There she loot it hing for a year and a day,
But oh! how looked her a—e when her c—t was away?

NAE HAIR ON'T.
Tune—*"Gillicrankie."*
An old fragment.

    Yestreen I wed a lady fair,
☐An ye wad believe me,
 On her c—t there grows nae hair,
☐That's the thing that grieves me.

 It vex'd me sair, it plagu'd me sair.
☐It put me in a passion,
 To think that I had wed a wife,
☐Whose c—t was out o' fashion.

THE SODGER LADDIE.
Tune—*"Sodger Laddie."*

This is the "tozie drab's" song in the "Jolly Beggars," found in every modern edition of the Poet's works. I once was a maid, though I cannot tell when,
And still my delight is in proper young men;
Some one of a troop of dragoons was my daddie,
No wonder I'm fond of a sodger laddie.

☐Sing, lal de lal, &c.

The first of my loves was a swaggering blade,
To rattle the thundering drum was his trade;
His leg was so tight, and his cheek was so ruddy,
Transported I was with my sodger laddie.

☐Sing, lal de lal, &c.

But the godly old chaplain left him in the lurch,
The sword I forsook for the sake of the church;
He ventured the soul and I risked the body—
'Twas then I proved false to my sodger laddie.

☐Sing, lal de lal, &c.

Full soon I grew sick of my sanctified sot,
The regiment at large for a husband I got;
From the gilded spontoon to the fife I was ready,
I asked no more but a sodger laddie.

☐Sing, lal de lal, &c.

But the peace it reduced me to beg in despair,
Till I met my old boy at a Cunningham fair;
His rags regimental they fluttered so gaudy,
My heart it rejoiced at a sodger laddie.

☐Sing, lal de lal, &c.

And now I have lived—I know not how long,
And still I can join in a cup and a song;
But whilst with both hands I can hold the glass steady,
Here's to thee, my hero, my sodger laddie!

☐Sing, lal de lal, &c.

O GIN I HAD HER.
Tune—*"Saw ye na my Peggy."*
An old fragment.

O gin I had her,
O gin I had her,
O gin I had her,
  Black altho' she be;
I wad lay her bale,
I'd gar her spew her kail;
She ne'er sou'd keep a meal,
  Till she dandl'd it on her knee.

She says I am light
 To manage matters right,
 That I've nae might or weight
  To fill a lassie's pock;
 But wad she tak' a yokin',
 I'd soon set her a bockin',
 I'd set a cradle rockin',
  Wi' a sample o' the stock.

THE LASSIE GATH'RING NITS.
Tune—*"O the broom."*
An old song.

There was a lass, and a bonie lass,
　A gath'ring nits did gang;
She pu'd them heigh, she pu'd them laigh,
　She pu'd them whare they hang.

Till tir'd at length, she laid her down,
　An' sleept the wood amang;
When by there cam three lusty lads,
　Three lusty lads an' strang.

The first did kiss her rosy lips,
　He thought it was nae wrang;
The second lous'd her bodice fair,
　Fac'd up wi' London whang.

An' what the third did to the lass,
　Is no' put in this sang;
But the lassie wauken'd in a fright,
　An' says, I hae sleepit lang.

THE LINKING LADDIE.
Tune—*"Push about the jorum."*
An old fragment.

Waes me that e'er I made your bed!
 Waes me that e'er I saw ye!
For now I've lost my maidenhead,
 An' I ken na how they ca' ye.

My name's weel kend in my ain countrie,
 They ca' me the linkin' laddie;
An' ye had na been as willing as I,
 Shame fa' them wad e'er hae bade ye.

TAIL TODLE.
Tune—*"Charlie's muster roll"*
An old song.

Tail todle, tail todle,
Tammie gart my tail todle
But an' ben wi' diddle doddle,
Tammie gart my tail todle.

Our gudewife held o'er to Fife,
For to buy a coal riddle;
Lang or she came back again,
Tammie gart my tail todle.

Tail todle, &c.

When I'm dead I'm out o' date;
When I'm sick I'm fu' o' trouble;
When I'm weel I stap about,
And Tammie gars my tail todle.

Tail todle, &c.

Jenny Jack she gae a plack,
Helen Wallace gae a boddle;
Quo' the bride, it's o'er little
For to mend a broken doddle.

Tail todle, &c.

DUNCAN GRAY.

An old song. Burns's purified version is well known. Another version, beginning "Weary fa' ye, Duncan Gray," more on the lines of the original, is ascribed erroneously by some editors to Burns. It will be found in Scott Douglas's Kilmarnock Edition (Vol. I., p. 221).

Can ye play me Duncan Gray,
　Ha, ha, the girdin' o't,
O'er the hills an' far awa',
　Ha, ha, ha, the girdin' o't.
Duncan came our Meg to woo,
Meg was nice and wadna do,
But like an ether puff'd and blew
　At offer o' the girdin' o't.

Duncan, he cam' here again,
　Ha, ha, the girdin' o't.
A' was out an' Meg her lane,
　Ha, ha, ha, the girdin' o't.
He kiss'd her butt, he kiss'd her ben,
He bang'd a thing against her wame;
But, troth, I now forget its name,
　But, I trow, she gat the girdin' o't.

She took him to the cellar then,
　Ha, ha, the girdin' o't,
To see gif he could do't again,
　Ha, ha, the girdin' o't.
He kiss'd her ance, he kiss'd her twice,
An' maybe Duncan kiss'd her thrice,
Till deil a mair the thing wad rise,
　To gie her the lang girdin' o't.

But Duncan took her to his wife,
　Ha, ha, the girdin' o't.
To be the comfort o' his life,
　Ha, ha, the girdin' o't.
An' now she scauls baith night an' day,
Except when Duncan's at the play;
An' that's as seldom as he may,
　He's weary o' the girdin' o't.

JOHNIE SCOTT.
Tune—*"O the broom."*
An old fragment.

Where will we get a coat to Johnie Scott,
  Amang us maidens a'?
 Whare will we get a coat to Johnie Scott,
  To mak' the laddie braw;
 There's your c—t hair, and there's my c—t hair,
 An' we'll twine it wondrous sma';
 An' if waft be scarce, we'll cow our a—e,
  To mak' him kilt an' a'.

I AM A BARD.
Tune—"*For a' that, and a' that.*

This is the song of "the wight o' Homer's craft" in the "Jolly Beggars."   I am a bard of no regard
Wi' gentle folks, and a' that;
But Homer-like, the glowrin' byke,
Frae town to town I draw that.

For a' that, and a' that,
And twice as muckle's a' that;
I've lost but ane, I've twa behin'—
I've wives eneugh for a' that.

I never drank the Muses' stank,
Castalia's burn, and a' that;
But there it streams, and richly reams,
My Helicon I ca' that.

For a' that, &c.

Great love I bear to a' the fair,
Their humble slave, and a' that;
But lordly will, I hold it still
A mortal sin to thraw that.

For a' that, &c.

In raptures sweet, this hour we meet,
Wi' mutual love, and a' that;
But for how lang the flie may stang,
Let inclination law that.

For a' that, &c.

Their tricks and craft have put me daft.
They've ta'en me in, and a' that;
But clear your decks, and here's—"The Sex!"
I like the jads for a' that.

For a' that, and a' that,
　And twice as muckle's a' that;
　My dearest bluid to do them gude.
　They're welcome till't for a' that.

FOR A' THAT AN' A' THAT.

This version did not appear in the original Crochallan edition. It appeared in a very early edition of the spurious "Merry Muses," and we print it in italics because it is much in the vein of "The Patriarch."

The boniest lass that ye meet neist,
Gie her a kiss an' a' that,
In spite o' ilka parish priest,
Repentin' stool, an' a' that.
For a' that an' a' that.
Their mim-mou'd sangs an' a' that,
In time and place convenient.
They'll do't themselves for a' that.

Your patriarchs, in days o' yore.
Had their handmaids an' a' that;
O' bastard gets, some had a score.
An' some had mair than a' that.
For a' that an' a' that,
Your langsyne saunts, an' a' that,
Were fonder o' a bonie lass,
Than you or I, for a' that.

King Davie, when he waxed auld,
An's bluid ran thin an' a' that,
An' fand his c—s were growin' cauld,
Could not refrain, for a' that.
For a' that an' a' that,
To keep him warm, an' a' that.
The daughters o' Jerusalem
Were waled for him, an' a' that.

Wha wadna pity thae sweet dames
He fumbled at, an' a' that,
An' raised their bluid up into flames,
He couldna drown, for a' that.
For a' that an' a' that,
He wanted pith, an' a' that;
For, as to what we shall not name,
What could he do, but claw that.

King Solomon, prince o' divines,
Wha proverbs made, an' a' that,
Baith mistresses an' concubines.
In hunders had, for a' that.
For a' that an' a' that,

Tho' a preacher wise, an' a' that,
The smuttiest sang that e'er was sung,
His "Sang o' Sangs" is a' that.

Then still I swear, a clever chiel
Should kiss a lass, an' a' that,
Tho' priests consign him to the deil,
As reprobate, an' a' that.
For a' that, an' a' that.
Their canting stuff, an' a' that.
They ken nae mair wha's reprobate,
Than you or I, for a' that.

MY WIFE'S A WANTON WEE THING.

 An old song which appears in Herd's Collection. Burns amended it in his lyric beginning, "She is a winsome wee thing."   My wife's a wanton wee thing,
 My wife's a wanton wee thing,
 My wife's a wanton wee thing,
 She winna be guided by me.

 She play'd the loon or she was married,
 She play'd the loon or she was married.
 She play'd the loon or she was married.
 She'll do it again or she die.

 She sell'd her coat and she drank it,
 She sell'd her coat and she drank it;
 She row'd hersel' in a blanket,
 She winna be guided by me.

 She mindit na when I forbad her.
 She mindit na when I forbad her,
 I took a rung and I claw'd her,
 An' a braw good bairn was she.

HE TILL'T AND SHE TILL'T.
Tune—"*Maggie Lauder*."
An old fragment.

He till't and she till't,
　And a' to make a lad again;
But the auld held, feckless carle,
　Soon began to nod again.

And he dang, and she flang.
　And a' to mak' a lassie o't;
And he bor'd and she roar'd.
　But they couldna mak' a lassie o't.

MADGIE CAM TO MY BEDSTOCK.

Tune—*"Clout the Cauldron."*

An old fragment.

Madgie cam to my bedstock,
To see gif I was waukin;
I pat my han' atweesh her feet,
An' fand her wee bit maukin.

Fal, lal, &c.

C—t it was the sowen-pat.
An' p—t—e was the ladle;
B—l—ks were the serving men
That waited at the table.

Fal, lal, &c.

TWEEDMOUTH TOWN.
An old song apparently of English origin.

Near Tweedmouth town there liv'd three maids,
  Who used to tope good ale;
 An' there likewise there liv'd three wives,
  Who sometimes wagged their tail;
 They often met to tope an' chat,
  An' tell odd tales of men;
 Cryin' when shall we meet again an' again,
  Cryin' when shall we meet again.

 Not far from these there liv'd three widows,
  With complexions wan and pale,
 Who seldom used to tope an' bouse,
  An' seldom wagged their tail.
 They sigh'd, they pin'd, they griev'd, they whin'd,
  An' often did complain,
 Shall we, quo' they, ne'er sport or play,
  Nor wag our tails again an' again,
  Nor wag our tails again.

 Nine northern lads with their Scots plads,
  By the Union, British call'd,
 All nine inch men, to a bousing came,
  Wi' their brawny backs I'm tald.
 They all agreed to cross the Tweed,
  An' ease them of their pain;
 They laid them all down,
 An' they f——d them all round,
  An' crossed the Tweed again an' again,
  An' crossed the Tweed again.

WHA IS THAT AT MY BOWER DOOR.

This is by Burns. It appears in most editions of his published works.

Wha is that at my bower door?
☐O wha is it but Findlay!
Then gae your gate, ye'se nae be here;
☐Indeed maun I! quo' Findlay:
What mak ye, sae like a thief?
☐O come and see! quo' Findlay:
Before the morn ye 'll work mischief;
☐Indeed will I! quo' Findlay.

Gif I rise and let you in;
☐Let me in! quo' Findlay:
Yell keep me wauken wi' your din;
☐Indeed will I! quo' Findlay:
In my bower if ye should stay;
☐Let me stay! quo' Findlay:
I fear ye'll bide till break o' day;
☐Indeed will I! quo' Findlay.

Here this night if ye remain;
☐I'll remain! quo' Findlay:
I dread ye'll learn the gate again;
☐Indeed will I! quo' Findlay.
What may pass within this bower:
☐Let it pass! quo' Findlay:
Ye maun conceal till your last hour;
☐Indeed will I! quo' Findlay.

COME COW ME MINNIE.
Tune—"*My mither's aye glowrin' o'er me.*"

A letter to Robert Cleghorn, dated October 25, 1793 (formerly quoted), thus concludes—
"Mair for token, a fine chiel—a hand-waled friend and crony o' my ain, gat o'er the lugs in love
wi' a braw, bonie, fodgel hizzie i' the burgh of Annan, by the name o' 'Bonie Mary,' and I tauld
the tale as follows: (N.B.—The chorus is auld).

"'Come cow me, minnie, come cowe me.'
"Tune—'*My minnie's aye glowerin' o'er me.*'

Forgive this wicked scrawl. Thine in all the sincerity of a brace of honest port.—R.B."

 □Come cow me minnie, come cow me;
□Come cow me minnie, come cow me;
□The hair o' my a—e is grown into my c—t,
□An' they canna win in for to mow me.

When Mary cam o'er the Border,
When Mary cam o'er the Border,
In troth 'twas approachin' the c—t of a hurchin,
Her a—e was in sic a disorder.
 □Come cow me, &c.
 But wanton Wattie cam west on't,
But wanton Wattie cam west on't,
He did it sae tickle, he left nae as meikle,
As a spider wad biggit a nest on't.
 □Come cow me, &c.
 An' was nae Wattie a blinker,
He m—w'd frae the queen to the tinkler;
Then sat down in grief like the Macedon chief,
For want o' mae warlds to conquer.
 □Come cow me, &c.
 But oh, what a jewel was Mary!
An' what a jewel was Mary,
Her face it was fine an' her bosom divine,
An' her c—t it was theekit wi' glory.
 □Come cow me, &c.

Note.—The most of the foregoing pieces are printed
in   "MERRY SONGS AND BALLADS
prior to the year a.d. 1800,
edited by
John S. Farmer.
Privately Printed for Subscribers only.

MDCCCXCVII."

       The notes which accompany the text in that work
give no clue whereby their authenticity may be
ascertained.

THE
COURT OF EQUITY;
OR,
THE LIBEL SUMMONS.
BY
ROBERT BURNS.

(COMPLETE VERSION).

Collated from the British Museum MSS. and other Sources.

THE COURT OF EQUITY.

INTRODUCTION.

This youthful *jeu de'sprit* of the poet was composed in the Spring of 1786, before the publication of his poems brought him prominently before the world. At that time, his relations with Jean Armour, coupled with his former error with Elizabeth Paton, servant maid to the household at Lochlie, afforded ample material for the gossips and scandalmongers of Mauchline to "tease his name in kintra clatter." Along with his friends—John Richmond, law clerk; James Smith, merchant; and William Huner, shoemaker—all then resident in the village—he established a bachelors' club, which held stated meetings in the "Whitefoord Arms," a hostelry kept by John Dove, the "Johnie Doo" and "Johnie Pigeon" to whom he refers in other connections. One of the self-imposed duties of this secret association was humorously given out to be the supplementing of the efforts of the Kirk Session by searching out and bringing to book all transgressors who cultivated the "better art o' hiding." The poem professedly describes one of the sittings of this bachelors' club, at which it had constituted itself a "Court of Equity" for the trial of two alleged offenders—"Sandy," or "Coachman Dow," and "Jock," or "Clockie Brown"—against each of whom a "Libel Summons" was issued, in comical imitation of a regular court of law, Burns being designated president; Smith, fiscal; Richmond, clerk; and Hunter, messenger-at-arms.

Judging from the MS. copies which have been preserved, it does not appear that a final corrected copy was ever executed by the poet. That the piece is imaginary in some of its details is proved by the fact that John Richmond left Mauchline for Edinburgh about November, 1785. A version is preserved in the British Museum among the Egerton manuscripts; and in the same collection are to be found a fragment of the same version, and a curtailed version known as the "Additional MS."[1] Besides these, Mr. Scott Douglas evidently had access to another version, MS. copies of which he distributed amongst his friends when engaged on his *magnum opus*, the Edinburgh edition of the works of the poet. Concerning the origin of that version we have no information. In the transcript given here, we found upon Scott Douglas's version,[2] and indicate the differences and variation of the text as established by comparison.

An incomplete version of the "Court of Equity" seems to have been first published *circa* 1810 in octavo sheet form. It also appears surreptitiously appended to certain editions of the works of the poet about the same date. We have seen a copy of it in an appendix to an Alnwick edition, *circa* 1810. In 1827 it was printed in that filthy receptacle, "The Merry Muses"—the volume with which the name of Burns has been so erroneously and unjustly associated, and it is still retained in the ever-recurring issues of the obscenities therein contained. In 1893, an expurgated version was published in the Aldine edition, under the editorship of Mr. G. A. Aitken. Scott Douglas quotes the opening lines in his Kilmarnock edition, and again refers to the production in his Edinburgh edition (Vol. I., pp. 163, 166). Robert Chambers thus refers to it— "He composed, on the 4th of June, a poem on the reigning scandals of his village, cases on which the Session Record throws ample light, if light were of any use in the matter; but, unfortunately, though the mock-serious was never carried to a greater pitch of excellence than in this poem, its license of phrase renders it utterly unfit for publication." To this Dr. Wallace, in his new edition of Chambers, appends—"The composition is full of tenderness and humanity, but it is too 'broad' for publication."

Concerning the *dramatis personæ* Richmond was law clerk with Gavin Hamilton before he removed to Edinburgh, and it was in his lodgings that Burns found accommodation during his first visit to that city. He spent the last years of his life in Mauchline, and died there in 1846. Smith, to whom he addresses one of his epistles, was a draper in his native town who started an unsuccessful calico printing business in Lesmahagow, and ultimately died in Jamaica. Hunter was the village shoemaker, of whom no mention is made save in this effusion. The worthy trio, it appears, had each had experience of the pains and penalties which attached to personal appearance before the Kirk Session of Mauchline, hence their selection by the poet as the accredited officials of the mock tribunal. Sandy Dow (son of John Dow or Dove, mine host of the "Whitefoord Arms") drove the coach between Mauchline and Kilmarnock, hence his *soubriquet* of "Coachman." John Brown ("Clockie Brown") was watch and clockmaker in the village, and the hero of "Lament him, Mauchline husbands a'," which is dedicated to "Johannis Fuscus," in the original MS. The harder terms meted out to him seem to have been because of the aggravations condescended upon, and because he was not, like Dow, a brother "of the mystic tie" of Freemasonry. Of the heroines, nothing of certainty is known of Jeanie Mitchell. Maggie Borland was the daughter of the landlord of another hostelry, "The Red Lion." The "Godly Bryan" and his particular transgression are referred to in a paragraph, sometimes omitted, from Burns's letter to John Richmond, of July 9, 1786. "Godly Bryan was in the *Inquisition* yesterday, and half the countryside as witnesses against him. He still stands out steady and denying; but proof was led yesternight of circumstances highly suspicious, almost *de facto:* one of the girls made oath that she upon a time rashly entered the house (to speak in your cant) 'in the hour of cause.'" As a matter of fact, Bryan, farmer, West Welton, did actually appear before the Session of Mauchline on July 8, 1786, to answer to a charge of immorality preferred against him. He died at Mauchline, and is buried in the churchyard there. The scene of Brown's imaginary punishment was the village green, in the centre of which then stood the village pump, a handy stake to which to tie the culprit, while the populace energetically expressed their opinion of him in the literal way which then obtained.

By the aid of these brief notes, it will be found that the poem sufficiently explains itself.

In Truth and Honour's name—Amen!
Know all men by these presents plain,
The Fourth o' June,[3] at Mauchline given,
The year 'tween eighty-five and seven,
We, old practitioners,[4] by profession,
As per extracts frae Books o' Session,[5]

In way and manner here narrated,
All *con amore*[6] congregated,
Are, by our brethren, constituted
A Court of Equity deputed,
With special authorised direction,
To take within our strict protection,
The open stay-laced[7] *quondam* maiden,
With growing life and anguish laden,
Who, by the miscreant,[8] is denied,
That led her thoughtless steps aside;
He who disowns the ruined fair one,
And for her wants and woes does care none;[9]
The wretch who can deny subsistence,
To life he rak'd into existence;[10]
The coof wha stands on clishmaclaver,
When lassies halflins offer favour;[11]
The sneak wha at a lassie's by-job,
Defrauds her wi' a frig or dry-bob;[12]
The knave, wha takes a private stroke,
Beneath a sanctimonious cloak;
In short, all who in any manner,[13]
Shall stain the fornicator's honour;
To take cognisance thereanent,
And punish the impenitent,[14]
We are the judges competent.

First Poet Burns he takes the chair,
Allow'd by a' his title's clear;[15]
He shows a duplicate pretension,[16]
To pass *nem. con*, without dissension:
Neist, Merchant Smith, our trusty Fiscal,
To cow each pertinacious rascal,
For whilk, his very foes admit,[17]
His merit is conspicuous great;
Richmond, the third, our worthy clerk,
Our minutes he will duly mark,[18]
And sit, dispenser o' the law,
In absence o' the ither twa;[19]
And fourth, our messenger-at-arms,
When failing a' the milder terms,
Hunter, a hearty willing brither,
Weel skilled in dead and livin' leather.
Without preamble, less or mair said,
We—body politic—aforesaid,
For sake o' them for whom and wherefore[20]
We are appointed here to care for,

Shall punish contravening truants,
At instance of our constituents,
And under proper regulation
Amend the lists of fornication.[21]

Whereas our fiscal, by petition,
Informs us there is strong suspicion
That Coachman Dow and Clockie Brown,
Baith residenters in this toun—
In ither words, you, Jock and Sandy,
Hae been at warks o' houghmagandie;
And noo when facts are brought tae light,
Thae facts ye baith deny outright.[22]

First, Clockie Brown, there's witness borne,
And affidavit made and sworn,
That ye hae wrought a hurly-burly,[23]
In Jeanie Mitchell's turlie-whurlie,
And graizl'd[24] at her regulator,
Till a' her wheels gang clitter-clatter;[25]
And, further still, you cruel Vandal—
A tale might e'en in hell be scandal—
That ye hae made repeated trials,[26]
Wi' drogs and draps in doctors' vials,
Mixed, as ye thought, in fell infusion,
Your ain begotten wean to poosion;
And yet ye are sae scant o' grace,
As daur to lift your brazen face,"[27]
And offer here to tak' your aith,[28]
Ye never lifted Jeanie's claith;
But though ye should yoursel' manswear[29]
Laird Wilson's sclates can witness bear,
Last Mauchline February Fair,[30]
That Jeanie's masts ye laid them bare,[31]
And ye had furled up her sails,[32]
And was at play at heads and tails.

Next, Sandy Dow, ye are indited,
As publicly ye hae been wyted,
For aft clandestinely upwhirlin'[33]
The petticoats o' Maggie Borlan',
And giein' her canister a rattle,
That months hereafter winna settle;[34]
And yet, ye loon, ye still protest[35]
Ye never harried Maggie's nest,

Tho' its weel ken'd that at her gyvil,[36]
Ye've dune what time will soon unravel.

Sae, Brown and Dow, above designed
For clags and claims hereto subjoined,[37]
The Court aforesaid cite and summon,
That on the fourth o' July comin',[38]
The hour o' cause, in our Court-ha',
The Whitefoord Arms, ye'll answer a';[39]
Exculpate proof ye needna bring,
For we're resolved about the thing;[40]
Yet, as reluctantly we punish,
And rather would with zeal admonish,[41]
Since better punishment prevented,
Than obstinacy sair repented,[42]
We, for that ancient secret's sake
Ye have the honour to partake,
And for that noble badge you wear,
You, Sandy Dow, our brither dear,
We give you as a man and mason,
This serious, sober, frien'ly lesson;
Your crime—a manly deed we trow it,
For men, and men alone, can do it,
And he's nae man that won't avow it;[43]
Therefore, confess, and join our core,
And keep reproach outside the door,
For in denial persevering,
Is to a scoundrel's name adhering;[44]
The best o' men hae been surprised,
The doucest women been advised,
The cleverest lads hae had a trick o't,
The bonniest lasses ta'en a lick o't,
Kings hae been proud our name to own,[45]
As adding glory to their crown,
The rhyming sons o' bleak Parnassus,
Were aye red-wud about the lasses,
And saul and body baith would venture,
Rejoicing in our lists to enter,
E'en (wha wad trow't), the cleric order,
Aft slyly break the hallowed border,
And show, in kittle time and place,
They are as scant o' boasted grace
As ony o' the human race:
So, Sandy Dow, be not ashamed
In sic' a quorum to be named;[46]

See, even himsel'—there's godly Bryan,[47]
The auld whatreck, he has been tryin';
When such as he put tae their han',
What man on character need stan'?
Then lift an honest face upon it,
When in a fau't, it's best to own it,
"I, Sandy Dow, gat Meg wi' wean,"
"An's just as fit to do't again;"[48]
Ne'er mind their solemn reverend faces,
Had they, in proper times and places,
But seen and fun'—I muckle dread it,
They just would dune as you and we did;
To tell the truth's a manly lesson,
An' doubly proper in a mason.[49]

For you, Jock Brown, sae black your fau't is,
Sae doubly dyed—we gi'e you notice,[50]
Unless you come to quick repentance,[51]
Acknowledge Jean's and your acquaintance,
Remember this shall be your sentence:—
Our beagles[52] to the Cross will tak' ye,
And there shall mither-naked mak' ye,
Some cannie grip near by your middle,
They shall it bind as tight's a fiddle,[53]
The rape they round the pump shall tak',[54]
And tie your han's ahint your back,
Wi' just an ell o' string allowed,
To jink and hide ye frae the crowd,
There shall ye stand—a lawfu' seizure,
Enduring Jeanie Mitchell's pleasure,
Sae be her pleasure don't surpass,[55]
Five turnings o' a half-hour glass,[56]
Nor will it in her pleasure be,
To turn you loose in less than three.
This our *futurum esse* decreet,
We mean not to be kept a secret,
But in our summons here insert it,
And whoso dares let him subvert it;[57]
Thus, marked above, the date and place is,
Sigillum est, per Burns, the praeses,
This summons, wi' the signet mark,[58]
Extractum est, per Richmond, Clerk;[59]
At Mauchline, *idem* date of June,[60]
'Tween four and five of afternoon,
You twa, *in propria persona*,
Before designed, Sandy and Johnie,

This summons legally ye've got it,
 As *vide* witness undernoted,[61]
 Within the house of John Dow, vintner.
Nunc facio hoc, Gulielmus Hunter.

↑ Referred to in the textual notes as Eg. Ver., "Frag. MS.," and "Add. MS."

↑ Referred to as "S.D.'s version."

↑ This twalt o' May.—Eg. Ver. 4th of June,—Add. MS.

↑ We, fornicators.—Eg. Ver.

↑ As per *extractum* from each Session.—Eg. Ver.

↑ *Pro bono amor.*—Add. MS.

↑ The stays unlacing.—Eg. Ver. The stays outbursting.—Add. MS.

↑ Scoundrel, Eg. Ver.—Rascal, Add. MS.

↑ This couplet found only in Add. MS.

↑ The wretch that can refuse assistance,
To those to whom he has given existence.

↑ This couplet found only in the Frag. MS.

↑ This couplet found only in S. D.'s Version.

↑ All who in any way or manner.—Eg. Ver.

↑ This line omitted in Egerton Version.

↑ "Fair."—Eg. Ver.

↑ An allusion to his two lapses.

↑ In this, as every other state.—Eg. Ver.

↑ Our minutes regular to mark.—Eg. Ver.

↑ "Former twa."—Eg. Ver.

↑ With legal due whereas and wherefore.—Eg. Ver.

↑ There is a slight variation of this quartette in the Egerton Version.

↑ The matter ye deny outright.—Eg. Ver.

↑ That ye hae raised.—Eg. Ver. That ye hae bred.—Add. MS.

↑ "Bloostr'd" in some printed copies.

↑ This couplet is found in S. D.'s version alone.

↑ Ye've made repeated wicked trials.—Eg. Ver.

↑ Ye daur set up.—Eg. Ver.

↑ And offer for to tak'.—Eg. Ver.

↑ But though by heaven and hell ye swear.—Eg. Ver.

↑ Ae e'enin' o' a Mauchline fair.—Eg. Ver.

↑ They saw them bare.—Eg. Ver.

↑ For ye had.—Eg. Ver.

↑ To have, as publicly ye're wyted,
Been clandestinely upward whirlin'.—Eg. Ver.

↑ That months to come it.—Eg. Ver.

↑ And yet ye offer your protest.—Eg. Ver.

↑ Ye hae gi'en mony a kytch and kyvil.—Eg. Ver.

↑ For clags and clauses there subjoined.—Eg. Ver.

↑ That on the 4th o' June incomin'.—Eg. Ver.

↑ Ye answer law.—Eg. Ver.

↑ This couplet is found only in S. D.'s Ver.

↑ And rather mildly would admonish.—Eg. Ver.

↑ This couplet is found only in the Eg. Ver.

↑ This line is awanting in the Eg. Ver.

↑ This couplet is found only in the Eg. Ver.

↑ This and the ten lines immediately following are found only in S. D.'s Ver.

↑ In the Eg. Ver. this runs—

Then, Brother Dow, if you're ashamed,
In such a quorum to be named,
Your conduct much is to be blamed.

↑ This and the three following lines are only found in the Eg. Ver.

↑ In the Eg. Ver. this runs—

Then, Brither Dow, lift up your brow,
And, like yoursel', the truth avow,
Erect a dauntless face upon it,
And say, "I am the man has done it,"
"I, Sandy Dow, gat Meg wi' wean,
An's fit to do as much again."

↑ The previous six lines are found only in the Eg. Ver.

↑ You, Monsieur Brown, as it is proven,
Jean Mitchell's wame by you was hoven.—Eg Ver.

↑ Without you by a quick repentance.—Eg. Ver.

↑ Beadles.—Eg. Ver.

↑ This couplet found only in the Eg. Ver.

↑ Around your rump.—S. D.'s Ver.

↑ Dinna pass.—Eg. Ver.

↑ Seven turnings.—Eg. Ver.

↑ Whoso dares may controvert it.—Eg. Ver.

↑ In the Eg. Ver. the signature here appears "(L. S.) B....."

↑ Richmond's signature here appears "R....d."

↑ At Mauchline, twenty-fifth of May, about the twalt hour o' the day.—Eg. Ver.

↑ This summons legally have got,
As *vide* witness underwrote.—Eg. Ver.

The End

Made in the USA
Las Vegas, NV
29 December 2022

64395187R00079